The Red Hourglass

Salves of the New World :1

Ashley Capes

The Red Hourglass

Copyright © 2017 by Ashley Capes

Cover Illiustration: Nick Deligaris
Cover Design: Vivid Covers
Layout & Typeset: Close-Up Books

ISBN-978-0-9876231-9-5

www.ashleycapes.com

Published by Close-Up Books
Melbourne, Australia

For Brooke

Chapter 1

Thomas placed the final black stone on the burial cairn and stood back, shielding his eyes from the vicious sun. Faint trails of red dust whipped across the barren plain before the crumbling ruin. He sighed. *Is this all there is to the world, truly? Even here, so far from all the despair?*

"What is it, Thomas?"

Mia stood with her arms folded, sightless eyes staring across the desert, dark hair swirling in the breeze. Dust covered her vest and pants – even her hair bore traces of the fine red sand. Her willow-rifle rested against her hip, the slim weapon little more than a guide now, since they'd not come across any ammunition in weeks.

Thomas hefted their pack onto his shoulders, pot within thudding against his back, and moved to stand by her. He placed a hand on her shoulder and squeezed. "David said to follow the old river to *Esmeralda*, so that's what we'll do. He said she'll be able to help us."

Mia shook her head. "We don't even know what he meant."

"I know, but we have to keep walking."

She gripped the rifle and leant against his chest. "Don't be so calm all the time. We're in trouble, you big fool; we're running out of water and Williams is probably still following us."

He put an arm around her, sleeve riding up his forearm to reveal the ugly yellow hourglass tattoo. Borrowed time – the slave's mark. "King Williams is probably miles away. I doubt he even knew which way to follow."

"Don't call him that; he's no king."

"I know that too, sis." He sighed again. "Did you want a moment?"

She pulled back, offering a small smile. Her green eyes grew wet when she faced the general direction of the cairn. "No. I said goodbye when he was still lucid."

"Then we'll leave him to the sand."

Mia turned away, starting without him, the rifle clicking against the few stones remaining in the sandy earth. Thomas looked to the cairn once more, the ribbons of granite shimmering in the dark stone.

Beneath lay the only man who'd protected them, a bright man, a noble man in spite of his oft-times mischievous sense of humour. "I'm sorry, David," he said. In the end, the old fellow had been losing hold of the present but at least Mia had been able to calm him with her singing, usually an ancient lullaby. *Maybe we failed him today but not tomorrow. Whoever Esmeralda is, we'll find her.*

"Thomas!"

He spun. Mia stood a little ways away, feet braced, rifle gripped in her hands. Thomas ran to her side, sliding in the sand. "What's wrong?"

"I hear something. It's distant, but it's the sand-hog, I'm sure of it."

"Then that bastard has caught up with us," Thomas said as he turned a circle, scanning the horizon. A dust cloud billowed up behind the wavering heat-lines that marred the earth. "There's his dust."

"How far?"

He grunted. "Williams will be upon us by sunset. Maybe before if they've guessed our path."

"Then we'd better hurry." She held out a hand.

He took it and together they broke into a jog.

***

The giant blue sky was melting down to orange at the horizon; shadows crept across the sand as Thomas came to a halt, Mia pausing beside him. One shadow had seemed to be cast by an eagle or falcon but when he glanced up, there was no trace of any bird. Was the heat making him imagine things? The huge, twin-peaked mountain thrusting up from the flat desert was no illusion, however. Still distant, it was taller than... than anything he'd ever seen. It dwarfed the shells of the tallest buildings left behind by his forefathers.

He glanced over his shoulder; the clouds from the hog neared.

"I feel something vast," Mia said.

"A mountain, like two cupped hands rising from the sand," he replied. "I think there's something at its base, too. We need to get closer." He strode forward. Mia followed, her rifle still preceding her, searching for obstacles. But the sand remained clear as it had for the entire afternoon; stunted, thin plants were few and far between, and stones had long since disappeared.

That was, until they neared the base and Thomas slowed, boots scraping on harder earth. "It's an ancient wreck – a steam train," he said.

Black iron absorbed what was left of the light beneath the mountain's shadow. The train bore a dozen carriages, all battered; many lay on their sides, half-buried in generations of sand. Red powder collected in the chimney and the windowsills, atop the wheels, smothering coupling rods, cloaking doors and hand rails. He described what he saw to his sister. "It's long abandoned; it might be a good hiding place."

"What else do you see?" Mia asked, her voice holding a note of concern.

He scratched at his stubble. "Little. It looks like we can access the first two carriages but the engine is pretty damaged. Farther on, I see the hint of an old rail; must have crashed a long time ago."

She gripped his arm. "Then you see no-one?"

A chill crept across his shoulders. *She feels something – friend or foe?* "Why? Do you sense danger?" He put a hand on the crow-bar swinging from his hip.

"Yes. No. Both – I can't explain it; I sense age, towering age. Something... I don't know. Just be ready."

"I will be."

The wind had died down and the rumble of the sand-hog grew louder, but there was still time to conceal themselves. Better yet, the steamer's passage would obliterate their tracks. Thomas unhooked his makeshift weapon as he neared the first carriage, glancing back to Mia. "I'll check."

"Be careful. And hurry."

He nodded. Even though she wouldn't have seen it, Mia knew he nodded, just as he knew she would be listening for any changes in the wind, vibrations in the earth or anything that prickled her sophisticated senses. He almost chuckled. *Whoever she inherited that from certainly didn't offer me anything special.*

His boots sank into the sand as he climbed, reaching for a handrail and hauling himself up to the door. The glass in the small square window was so thick and clouded with dust that it was impossible to penetrate. He gripped the handle and pulled.

Jammed.

Thomas applied more pressure, muscles straining. Still nothing. He set his crow-bar aside and placed his free hand on the carriage wall for leverage and tugged again. A screeching followed as the door shuddered open. Ducking away from the opening, he snatched up the bar and paused.

No sounds from within. Peering around the doorjamb, he saw little beyond the patch of light offered by the open door. Thomas glanced back to Mia. She stood as before, only now she hummed to herself. The ancient lullaby – the one she always hummed.

Behind her, the distant storm of red from the sand-hog filled the sky and the roar of its engines crossed the sand ahead of it. It would arrive before full dark.

We're running out of time.

He stepped into the stuffy room and moved to one side of the door. His eyes adjusted quickly. Rows of spacious seats, fabric rotted down to fragments, rested beneath dust-choked windows. Muted light fumbled its way within. Steel racks for overhead storage were empty even of cobwebs.

Rodent droppings, these too, long-since turned white with age, covered some of the tables and the sand that filtered into everything littered both sills and floor.

He moved down the aisle until he reached another door, which he wrenched open. Beyond lay the half-buried walkway between carriages. The huge bolt and clasp of the couplings connecting them peered from the red. The second carriage was just the same, only darker.

Mia's voice called, words indistinct.

Thomas rushed back to the first carriage, pausing at the doorframe.

She'd climbed half-way to the carriage. "Well?" she asked.

"Nothing amiss yet. It might serve as a hiding place," he said.

"Good."

He took Mia's outstretched hand and drew her into the shelter of the carriage. "Do you feel anything?"

"Nothing new... wait, I think –"

"Greetings, travellers."

An old man with a white beard and faded blue overalls stood in the open door at the far end of the carriage. A shovel rested against his shoulder and a cold lantern swung in one hand as he approached.

"Greetings." Thomas did not remove his hand from the crowbar, but neither did he lower it.

The old-timer slowed, stopping a few seats away. "You two seem like you're pretty far from home."

"How can you tell?" Mia asked softly.

He chuckled. "This is the end of the world, so I suppose everyone who comes here is far from home."

Thomas blinked. "The end of the world?"

"Well, it might as well be. Nothing much beyond the Praying Mountain but red sand and then endless cliffs. You must be thirsty, the both of you. I have water with me, outside."

Thomas glanced to his sister. She had not moved.

"You can trust old Garrett," he said. "I'm not going to harm you – but you'll need my help to hide from the sand-hog, believe me. The *Esmeralda* is the only shelter for miles and miles."

Thomas stepped forward. "Wait, are you saying this *train* is Esmeralda? Not a person. Not a place?"

"Right you are."

"We've been searching for it," Thomas said. "The man who raised us said –"

"No need to bore him with our life story," Mia interrupted. "Can you really help us, Garrett? Do you have weapons, a way to escape?"

"Just who's chasing you, girl?"

Mia gave a slight smile, as if being called 'girl' were amusing. Thomas almost smiled himself – they hadn't been children for years now. *Maybe orphans are never truly children, anyway.* Not that David had been a failure, but there was always something missing. Some sense that he and Mia came from somewhere else. And the years before David...

"Heard of 'King' Williams out here at the end of the world?" she asked.

Two white eyebrows shot up. "That's some real trouble."

"Then you'll know he doesn't like it when his slaves escape," Thomas said, holding up a wrist to reveal the hourglass.

Garrett squinted before sitting on the nearest seat, a humph-sound escaping as he did. "You're both yellows, huh?" He set the lantern on the back of the nearest headrest. "That's a little more than I'm used to dealing with, I have to admit. Palace slaves usually don't get so far."

"But you'll try help us anyway?" Thomas asked.

"I will. It'll have to be the last carriage," the old man said as he stood. "Williams won't be able to get in. Once he searches the other carriages and finds them empty, he'll likely give up."

"Maybe, maybe not," Mia said.

"Well, you'll have to take that risk. No other trains to hide in."

"So how do we get in?" Thomas asked.

Mia frowned. "Or out?"

"I'll show you, but first we need the key," Garrett said with a nod to himself. He led them back outside – moving swiftly despite a limp – to the setting sun where he circled the relic's engine and climbed its steps, grunting with the effort.

"Are you all right?" Thomas asked.

"The knees go first, lad."

A boiler dominated the room; large enough to house a whole family. The door stood open, the hinges rusted, and broken glass in the copper pressure-gauge caught the light. Nearby lay a collection of shovel heads, arranged on a stack of crates, all empty.

"I took the few remaining handles for my camp," Garrett said when he noticed Thomas looking at them.

Garrett slipped into the cab and rummaged about in a tin box, muttering to himself. Thomas followed. The room was barely large enough for two. Copper handles reached his knees beside a wide seat, the bulbs on their ends worn.

Through the dusty windows, the great wall of the mountain was darkening as the sun fell further.

"Here!" Garrett exclaimed. He held a heavy key up with a grin. "Thought I'd lost it."

Mia called from the boiler room. "That sand-hog will be here in moments, can we hurry things along?"

Chapter 2

As they passed the carriages, the old man offered them lukewarm goanna meat and water, which Thomas accepted gladly, despite craving a hot meal. Somehow, meat always tasted better right off the flame – even in a desert.

"We appreciate your kindness," Mia said between mouthfuls. "How long have you been here?"

"Months now." He wiped his brow. "There's old stories about this place, about what it used to be – holy land to the people who once lived here. I thought there might be treasure but I haven't found anything yet, bar a few cave paintings of snakes and lizards. And a giant bird; at first I thought it was drawn in gold paint." He chuckled. "I was wrong about that of course, but still, there's no time to shed tears over my rotten luck."

The last carriage rested some distance from the bulk of the *Esmeralda*, mostly up to its eaves in dark sand where it lay against the base of the mountain. The line of the long-buried train tracks curved in a half-circle, allowing a clear view of the train.

"How did it crash?" Mia asked. "This carriage is some distance from the others."

"Don't know, sad to say. Must have been a terrible day for the folks, so far away from help – this was well before the sand-hog and the like. Over a hundred years ago – pre-dates the Coal War, she does," Garrett explained as he climbed to the iron door. Its window, like all the others, was caked with dust. He brushed away a foot of sand at the base as best he could and inserted the key into the lock, ringed by an ornate brass sun.

When he swung the door open it revealed a second, heavier door, which was also locked. The same key admitted them into a large room lit by a narrow strip of light from where the roof had twisted free from the base; yet it illuminated little, leaving only an orange stripe on the wall opposite.

And more importantly, it was nothing anyone could squeeze through, by any means.

Mia gasped when she stepped inside and Thomas tensed. Danger? No, no. It hadn't been a gasp of fear... was it awe? Garrett knelt to light the lamp, winding a lever that clicked as it turned. Steady white light bloomed.

Thomas felt his own jaw drop open.

The room was full of caged birds. The light glinted on their steel wings and sharp beaks; the silver and gold plate alone had to be worth a kingdom, not to mention the gears and cogs that would surely lie within. Crystal gleamed in their tiny eyes, as if twinkling in sunlight.

All were identical.

"Robins," Thomas said softly.

"What is this place?" Mia asked Garrett. "I feel vast

potential here."

"Allow me," he said, and led her to a cage. "It's not dangerous."

She reached in, lifting a robin free to rest within her palm. Her face was full of wonder as she ran her fingertips across the intricate body, her worry-lines easing. Thomas swallowed; his chest swelled. *God, how long since I've seen her face look like that?*

The old man gestured to the birds. "I think an old king was transporting these treasures. Who knows? But not a single bird works. I've even taken one apart and all its pieces are in perfect order. There's just something missing; they're worthless to me."

"I recognise these," Mia said. "At least, I think I do. Thomas, do you remember the story David told us about the Royal Mechanical Birds? They were built for young princes and princesses, to emulate real birds."

"And that's what these are?" Thomas asked.

"Why not?"

"I suppose so." He couldn't help a grin. "I'd much prefer if they were guns. Or a steam-car."

A low rumbling rose then fell, as if the nearing steamer had crushed half-submerged stone. Its reinforced sides and heavy wedge would have dealt quite easily with the obstruction but the sound was a timely reminder.

"Stay here and you'll be fine," Garrett said, handing the key over and heading for the door.

"Where will you hide?" Thomas asked. "You could stay here."

"Yes, stay," Mia said.

He shook his head. "If they do search the area and find

my camp empty they'll be thorough instead of moving on. If they find me, I can send them on their way easily enough. They won't care about one crazy old man out in the desert."

Thomas frowned. "Williams isn't that reasonable."

"Don't worry, son. I have a few tricks up my sleeve. Now stay quiet, won't you?" He shut the outer door, which Thomas locked. Next came the inner door; its muted clang covered the sweeping that followed as Garrett obscured their tracks, muttering about his back as he worked.

Then his muffled voice grew distant and eventually the growl of the approaching sand-hog smothered it.

"I have to see. Be my eyes," Mia said.

Thomas arranged a pyramid with a few of the square cages, placing them beneath the gap in the roof, grunting as he lifted the heavy steel. Then he climbed atop and peered into the orange light.

Outside, the sand-hog bore down on the *Esmeralda*. The beastly machine sat two-storeys tall, and poured steam and smoke into the dusk from twin boilers. Orange light flashed off the reinforced windows in the engineers' box. Portholes for passengers – or in this case, soldiers – were closed. In battle, the great beast covered them with heavy blast shutters, rendering it immune to any rifle. Thomas had seen the heaviest shot leave naught but a mark on those shutters.

While the hog wasn't agile, such deficiency was offset by sheer power. Gatling guns flanked the steamer's top deck and sides, the gunners' platforms outfitted with heavy shields. Unmanned – for now.

Garrett was nowhere to be seen.

The steamer slowed as it approached the line of carriages, hissing and sending a spray of red sand forth like a wave.

The sand crashed over the *Esmeralda*, even the last carriage. Thomas flinched from it.

"What was that?" Mia asked, her voice tight.

"Just sand," he said, speaking softly. He straightened to peer back out. The new sand would cover any incidental tracks Garrett might have left too. Good. "The hog's stopped. The deck is still clear... wait, here they come."

A hatch flipped open with a clang that ricocheted off the mountain and rang across the desert.

Men in heavy flak jackets, with willow-rifles strapped to their backs, climbed out and took up positions at the Gatlings, while others scuttled down ladders to fan out before the steamer. More and more men followed, until it seemed no-one could possibly reside within the steamer anymore. *Too many.* No soldier approached the train but a woman's voice boomed from the large brass tube beside the cabin.

"In the name of King Williams, show yourselves. You are property of his kingdom; hide at your own peril."

Thomas shifted position on the cage. The voice was familiar.

"It's Elisabeth," Mia said. "Williams sent her after us – too lazy to come himself. Maybe we're not that valuable after all."

"She's still his second in command," Thomas said. And an uncompromising woman, too. A crack shot and far too clever, truly, to answer to Williams. Thomas nearly shrugged. *She probably has her reasons.*

Silence crossed the space between train and steamer.

"You test my patience," Elisabeth called.

No chance, lady.

Yet after a time, movement atop the steamer caught Thomas' eye. Men were manoeuvring a bulky gun into position. *Damn thing's huge.* The barrel seemed to be several feet wide. A thin trail of steam rose from the body. At the weapon's rear, men shovelled fuel into a small boiler, shouting about keeping an eye on the gauge.

He muttered a curse – a steam-cannon. Maybe Williams did want them after all. But why? *We're not* that *special, are we? They've got dozens of slaves in the Fortress and they can get more any time they want.*

"What is it?" Mia asked.

"They have some sort of steam-cannon. I didn't know they were safe enough to use yet."

"Now we do," she said, beginning to pace a small circle. "I don't like this. Can you see Garrett?"

"No. I don't think –"

Cries from the hog cut his words short. A boom rang out, a great explosion of hissing steam following as the cannon rocked back on its rail. Its shot hurtled into the first carriage like a thunderbolt, leaving a smoking hole in the caved-in side of the *Esmeralda*.

"Come out now or we will break every carriage open. If you make us come in and drag you out ourselves, you will become slaves with no hands – should you even survive. Do you understand?"

Thomas flinched. His heartbeat quickened. He looked back to Mia, whose expression was stony. Was surrender really an option? Too many years enslaved before David rescued them. *No.* Thomas clenched a hand. He remembered the taste of dirt all too well. *I can't go back.* And neither could Mia.

Again, commands rose from the sand-hog and the steam-cannon was shifted to aim at the next carriage. Steam began to hiss until another explosion rang out, smashing through the steel and glass effortlessly.

"Any ideas?" Thomas asked.

"Nothing yet," she said before taking a breath. She hummed as she stepped, her soothing voice at odds with the tension in his body.

"Damn it." Thomas sat atop one of the cages, head in his hands. There had to be something – maybe if they made a run for it between shots? How thick was the sand, truly? Maybe the cannon wouldn't even break the double walls of the last carriage... or maybe it would.

A new voice joined Mia's.

Thomas lifted his head.

"Do you hear that?" he asked.

His sister stopped. "What?"

"Hum again."

Mia repeated the melody, a simple rise and fall to the old lullaby, and was soon joined by a light chirping. *A bird?* Thomas strode across the room, examining the cages. "Keep going," he said. If the birds weren't truly broken, was there a chance they could buy their freedom?

Another shot crashed into the next carriage, a piece of steel clanging against their hiding place. "Louder," Thomas hissed.

Mia raised her voice – singing the words now, and one of the mechanical birds twitched. Its wing fluttered as it turned toward Mia, and it too matched her song.

A second hopped in its cage, and then a third. New chirping filling the room until a dozen voices had joined

Mia. Would Elisabeth and her men hear it? The lullaby was growing deafening now as the whole carriage joined in. He spun back to climb up to his perch, blinking against the light.

The men gathered around the sand-hog had not turned their way. Yet. But they were lining into formation; Elisabeth would soon send them to check the wreckage.

Mia paused to reach for him. "Thomas, you must close your eyes."

"Mia... what?"

"Please, I felt it before, I can call it to us. I can save us."

"What do you mean?"

The birdsong had swelled to an unpleasant pitch. Every single bird sang now, beaks flashing in the bright light... *Bright light?* He turned back toward the gap in the roof but an incandescent brightness from outside stopped him. He swore, ducking down to cover his head with his arms.

"Don't look until I tell you it's safe," Mia shouted over the song and then rejoined the chorus, her own voice soaring.

Thomas squeezed his eyes shut but the light bled into his mind.

Within the blackness of his eyelids a searing heat bloomed. A great white bird flared, wingtips aflame as it bore down on him.

Its beak opened in a shriek and it swept down to crash in an explosion of stars.

Something rocked the carriage walls.

Thomas flinched, but there was only the gradual fading of light and then silence, a silence soon broken by a soft sobbing. He opened his eyes, slowly. Then he lifted his head. The brilliance of the fire-bird was gone but a soft glow lingered, sneaking into the last carriage.

The mechanical birds had fallen silent.

Mia was weeping.

He stumbled to her, taking her face in his hands. "Mia, what..."

Mia's tears were streaked with blood and her green eyes stared directly into his own. "Thomas... I can see your outline," she said, and her smile was radiant. "You're fuzzy but you're there."

"I... *how?*" He barely spoke above a whisper.

"The Great Bird," she said, and then turned from the light. "God, it hurts so much more than I expected."

The bird of fire... or light – what was it? A deity once worshipped by the people Garrett mentioned? Those who hadn't left any relics behind? Thomas took his shirt and tore a strip free. "Here." Gently, he tied it around her head, covering her eyes. "Is that better?"

She nodded.

Thomas exhaled. "What now?"

Mia took his hand. "Now we leave, before the ones inside the steamer find us," she said.

Thomas paused to listen. Cries of despair and fear rose from outside. Voices shouting for help, shouting in pain. Confusion. Terror. He swallowed when he made out the words. "They're all blind," he said.

"Yes."

And finally something else dawned upon him.

His sister had called the bird of light; his sister had made the dead machines sing. Mia had used... magic... somehow. He exhaled. Magic. How? And what did it mean? Was that the reason Williams hounded them? Two slaves who'd been on the run for years? *Did David know all along?* Once again, Thomas wished there was someone who could tell him just who their parents had been.

Why they'd abandoned him and Mia.

And yet, as it always did, the question he could never answer only hardened his resolve. Mia had to be protected – that hadn't changed. Her vision might be restored but it was clear Williams would never stop chasing them.

Thomas looked back to Mia and smiled. *And I will never let him take her.*

Chapter 3

Thomas kicked the wheel of the broken-down jeep with a snarl.

Red dust swirled.

The sun pummelled his head and shoulders, and sweat trickled down his back. His ragged shirt clung to his skin as he pushed his sleeves back up, the bitter slave's mark catching his eye as it always did. *And I bet the prick who came up with that symbol was real proud of himself too.* Out here, so far from any city or settlement, there was no-one to see the tattoo on his forearm, and if they kept ahead of Elisabeth, no-one to try and drag him back to the hell he and Mia had once lived.

And no-one to stumble across and then rescue them either.

"Did kicking it make some diesel magically appear?"

Mia sat in the ripped passenger seat, face turned toward him. Her blindfold – the same piece of his shirt he'd torn only days before – held back her dark hair and protected her eyes from the sharpness of the desert sun. *Her vision's returning too slowly.* Still, it was better than nothing.

"No. But I feel a tiny bit better," he said.

"Good. Want to get back to our next move?"

He leant against the hot steel of the driver's door, staring across the red dunes. The stony rubble that passed for a road cut through the desert, disappearing into wavering mirage lines. "It's the same old move, isn't it?" he asked as he pushed himself from the door, now too hot to tolerate. "Walking."

"Yes, but which direction? Where are we now?"

He glanced over his shoulder. She was examining the willow rifle with her fingertips, searching for dents in the barrel. "Two days east of the *Esmeralda*'s wreck, I suppose. I thought we'd come across *something* but now I don't know. Why did David want us to find the train?"

"I don't know. I've been wondering."

"Maybe we should have tried to find Garret or head back toward the ruins at Springs. There was a well there at least."

"We made a choice," she said with a shrug. "No use second-guessing ourselves now."

He chuckled. "You still gonna think that if we die of thirst?"

"Ask me when we're facing that problem," she said, offering a smile of her own.

He turned and slapped the modest water tank in the backseat; a sloshing sound followed. "We'll be close enough if this runs out. Five days tops. And that's if Elisabeth doesn't catch up first."

Mia shook her head. "We've got a head start and most of them are blind now – I'm not worried about that lot."

"Still—"

"Thomas, I'm serious. We have to focus on what's in front

of us. You sabotaged the sand-hog and the other jeep, right? It's not like they'll come across any more fuel than we did."

He held up both hands, then realised the futility of it – blindfolded as she was. "Fine. You're right." *It was a big enough shock finding the jeeps in the first place.* 'King' Williams had certainly amassed quite the empire of relics somewhere. Jeeps with actual diesel. Scores of years since anyone had used diesel. Supposedly cheaper than steam but impossibly rare. How was the man producing it? Or was it an antique store?

"Thomas, are you listening?"

"Sorry."

"Come on, help me choose a direction."

"I'll do my best," he replied. "But can you... feel anything? Maybe if you try again?" He still didn't know how to describe the ability she possessed but her senses were far more sophisticated than even before. As if the Bird had changed or enhanced them. *Well, if it helps us now, I'll just have to call it a miracle, like before.*

She grinned. "I feel the sun singeing my hair."

"Give me a minute." He strode to the back of the jeep and pried open the toolbox. Within lay a tan-coloured tent. He lifted it free and started on the poles, stretching the canvas, pausing only to drive away a shining black scorpion, and soon enough, had Mia inside. She squeezed his hand when he sat in the scant shade the tent mouth cast. "How about now?"

"That's a little better." She sat cross-legged and rested her hands on her knees, exhaling slowly. "This didn't work before, you know."

He gave her hand a shake. "Try anyway."

Mia evened her breathing.

The sun continued to bore its way through the canvas and sweat trickled down Thomas' neck. "Anything?"

A furrow appeared in her brow and she waved his words away. Then she shook her head. "Something. It's no use to us, though."

"What did you see?"

"A rat in a suit."

He opened his mouth to reply but found no words at first. "I... what does that mean?"

She smiled. "If I knew, I'd tell you. But that's it. It was a rat. Standing in shadow, wearing a suit. Like we used to see in the Fortress. Remember the balls?"

He nodded. Mostly he remembered twisting between tables and chairs, lords and ladies in their flower-like colours as he balanced a tray of wine glasses with a rigid arm – fighting a trembling fear. The chef's voice echoed, even now, fifteen years later. *You drop another tray and you and your sister are finished, got it? Finished!* "Well, let's make a start. Which direction?"

"Let's just follow the road."

"All right." He started collecting their supplies and Mia moved around the front of the jeep, one hand trailing over the body as a guide. Over the armfuls of tent canvas, poles and rifles, he saw her pop the bonnet. More sabotage, no doubt.

When he had everything together, including the water, he joined her. "Don't forget this," he said, handing over her willow-rifle. She reached for it, taking it easily. Was her vision improving after all or was it just her old familiarity with him?

She led them along the road, the rifle used as a guide, but she rarely stumbled. He followed, casting glances over his shoulder, looking for dust on the horizon but nothing appeared.

By nightfall he let his aching arms and shoulders rest, sitting atop the water barrel. Mia waited at the crest of the depression, facing west where the sun had set. A new wind twisted the frayed edges of her vest. Heat was already seeping from the air, though it was still baked into the earth. "We're heading in the right direction," she said.

He looked up. "Yeah?"

"I feel it now. I still can't explain it though."

"So whatever your gift is doing, it's doing it properly now?"

She laughed, a sound that warmed his heart. "Well, I'm not even going to pretend I know how it works but I'm fairly confident. It's not like the rat."

His boots crunched over rubble as he joined her. She seemed confident and her gift hadn't let them down yet. "I trust you, sis."

Mia pointed. "By tomorrow, before noon. There's something out there."

"You know, old stories talk about a town out this way. On the edge of the world."

An eyebrow peeked above her blindfold. "Marwin? Where the ghost-people supposedly live?"

"Or maybe regular people who hid themselves away a long time ago. There's no rails this far north, and the road isn't much for steam-cars. I doubt Williams or even his father's men have been out here in decades."

"Why would they? There's nothing here."

"There was the *Esmeralda*."

"True."

"We won't know until tomorrow anyway. Let's get some rest."

"Good idea."

She took his hand as he helped her down the slope. At the bottom he started on the tent but paused to look at her. She drank from her flask, her blindfold facing the earth.

"I know it's dark now but... is your vision still getting better?" he asked. "Can you tell if there's a difference?"

A pause. "It's no better."

Some of the happiness he'd felt at hearing her laugh before slipped away. Perhaps the miracle back in the ancient steam train was not going to be as complete as he'd first believed. "Maybe something will change soon," he said.

She shrugged.

Thomas hid a sigh. It wasn't fair that she'd come so close to being cured of her blindness. *No. It's not unfair, it's cruel. What sort of miracle is only half a miracle?* Maybe Garrett could have explained it, but the old explorer had disappeared without a trace. Had he survived Elisabeth's attack?

"It's more light than I've known for years," she said, as if she could read his thoughts. "I'm not disappointed."

"I am," he said. "You deserve more."

She crossed the dusty earth and reached out, finding his shoulder. "Don't give up, we might find something better tomorrow. Whatever that... being of light did, it's for the better."

"At least we're still free." He did not add '*for now*', but he couldn't help looking past her calm face to the desert, where Elisabeth would no doubt be driving her soldiers after them, eager for revenge.

And still the same question returned to haunt him. *Why does King Williams want us so much? Is it Mia's power? How could he have known before we did?*

But the night gave no answer.

Chapter 4

Their footsteps echoed in the empty street.

Pale stone buildings stood streaked with red dust, worn deep into the pores. The sun pummelled the homes yet barely seemed to penetrate the black windows, long since empty of glass. The sharp scent of catweed lingered where the grey plant had forced its way up through the earth, lurking between building walls.

Thomas kept his rifle high as he led Mia toward a two-storey building in the centre of town; the only structure with a door, this made of steel. A wrought iron sign hung above, proclaiming a hotel. He stopped before it. "The White Tavern," he read aloud. "Maybe this place was Marwin maybe not."

He glanced at his sister; she held her own rifle, training it on the buildings behind them. Her head was tilted slightly, as if she were listening for movement. *Like before.* Her vision wasn't improving.

Thomas described the hotel. "It's the only place worth a look so far."

"Let's see," she said.

"I think we're alone here; I'm not sure we'll find anything useful."

"It's shelter if nothing else."

Thomas tried the handle and the door screeched open. He winced, glancing back into the street. No movement, nothing. "If there is anyone here, they'll know where we are now."

"So be it," Mia said.

He stepped inside, glancing around.

A wide reception area held a counter and the skeleton of two chairs, fabric rotted down to tatters. The open windows cast dim light across each surface, revealing a coating of fine red dust. The nearest door, this one of wood, led to a staircase and the other, behind the counter, to a cloak room. Empty shelves and hooks, and another door. He relayed what he saw to Mia.

"Looks like an office and a bedroom attached," he said.

She paused, a hand on the wall. "Upstairs?"

Thomas returned to the staircase, noting a narrow door off to the side, but continued climbing. Each step creaked, but held well enough. Were they reinforced? Not much else in the way of wood seemed solid here. Of course, Mia's footfalls were softer. So long as he didn't break the case before the top, she'd be fine.

"Just a hallway and a row of doors," he said once they stood together.

"Try one, I guess."

He pushed on the first door and the hinge gave way, wood crashing to the floor. Dust bloomed and he coughed, waving at it as he prodded at the floor with his rifle, then took a cautious first step inside. The floor seemed much more solid. A bed, empty of linen, lay against one wall and a tiny round table, also ravaged by dry rot, rested beneath a mirror on the opposite wall.

In the reflection, he was little more than a hulking blur.

But the room had a balcony, its iron rail, like everything else, coated in red dust. Thomas tested the platform, and finding it solid, stepped out.

"I feel air," Mia said. She stood near the bed, leaning against the willow-rifle.

"I'm on a balcony," he replied. "I can see the whole town."

Clusters of pale stone buildings stretched before him, their flat rooves may have once held gardens and canvas for shade, the empty poles perhaps a clue. Those closest were coated in desert-rust. Evenly spaced throughout the town rested squares with... he squinted... fountains in the centre.

"Is something wrong?" Mia asked. A note of concern had crept into her voice, as he'd been lax in sharing what he saw.

"No. It's just there's something in the squares." He explained. "I wonder if the fountains still work."

"Who would leave this place if it had water?"

"I know. But your feeling led us here. Maybe we should still—" He stopped. A new dust cloud was resolving on the horizon. Elisabeth. Impossible to tell how close – the question was: would she guess correctly once she found the jeep? "The sand-hog."

Mia swore as she straightened. "Close?"

"Not yet. It may not even be heading this way."

"Then we better find whatever it is we're supposed to find."

"*What*ever? Not someone?"

"No... I don't think it's a person."

He shrugged. "Let's finish with this place then and check one of those fountains."

"I'll wait here," Mia replied, a slight frown on her face. "I need to concentrate. It's almost as if there's... I can nearly feel it, Thomas."

"Will you be –?"

"Safe?" She grinned up at him. "Standing in one of the empty rooms of an abandoned inn? We've been in tighter spots, you know."

He chuckled. "I won't be far."

Thomas searched the rest of the rooms on their wing, finding little variation on the states of decay and emptiness. Only one room bore something of a possession, an old Christian symbol of the fish sat above the bed. Made of tin, it had been nailed to the cement between brickwork.

But it was the only thing he found. Even in the other wing, there remained no traces of human existence in the hotel aside from the dying furniture. In the kitchen he found naught but a cavernous oven and benches – like everywhere else, they held no clues as to why the town was empty.

After checking on Mia, he headed back down to the narrow door. He tried the handle. Locked. He took a step back, lined up his shoulder and rammed the door. It held. Thomas grunted as he lined it up again – he'd always been bigger and stronger than most folks; he'd once lifted a piece of fallen factory machinery so a friend could be pulled free. He wasn't going to let an old, wooden door stop him. He charged again. Wood splintered and he fell into a dark room. Very little light entered from windows in the staircase but it was enough to see a chest, half as tall as Thomas himself. A heavy padlock ensured it stayed closed. The leather coating was only worn, not yet disintegrating. Had it been treated? "Doesn't matter, does it?" he muttered to himself before heading back up the stairs to find Mia pacing the room.

"Anything?" he asked.

She shook her head. "I thought I had something but no. You?"

"There's a locked chest inside a locked room downstairs but I doubt it has water within."

"Hmmm." She turned to face the balcony. "Then we're back to your fountains. Or we head west again."

He moved to the balcony to check on the dust cloud – it was closer, perhaps not by much; he could not be sure as an approaching wind played with the cloud. But there was little doubt that time was running short once more.

"Let's see if the fountains are the reason we're here," he said.

Chapter 5

The fountain rested in the centre of the square, its sun-bleached tiles dry.

A low stone wall encircled it; deep-orange sand had built up on one side. The water-feature itself was a creature Thomas had never seen – heavy hind legs and a powerful tail, small forearms, and its head a mix somewhere between dog and rabbit. It was posed standing tall, at alert. The edges were chipped and worn with age but the carved illusion of fur was not ruined.

"I have not heard of such an animal," Mia said when he described it to her. She approached slowly. "But there's something here; this is different to the others. It's the right one."

"Water?"

"I don't know." Mia stopped at the low stone wall. She set her rifle and pack down then stepped into the fountain, fingers trailing the sculpture's face. "I get a sense of something ancient here, Thomas."

"Let's see." He set his own gear down and circled the

fountain. Was there any button or lever, some way to test its function? If the fountain did have access to some manner of underground stream, it might mean the difference between life and death. Admittedly, fountains were an odd thing for a desert town. Perhaps it had been built over a well. *Which doesn't make much sense either.*

He found nothing on the wall. But at the rear of the sculpture, halfway up the animal's back, Thomas spotted a circular opening broad enough to reach within. A small, tiled pattern ringed the opening, offering the impression that it was no accident. He stepped into the fountain and knelt by the hole. Steel glinted inside. "There's something here," he said.

Mia joined him, frowning when she ran her fingers over the surface then reached an arm inside. "There are evenly spaced, square holes within the shaft."

"For the water?" *Unlikely, surely.*

"No, there's a hole atop the animal's head for that. This must be how we operate the fountain."

"If it still works."

She nodded. "We need a key to find out – I'm betting that's what the square holes are for."

"Let's double check the other fountains, maybe we missed something."

But at each fountain they found no key and no more openings. Tension grew with each failure – Thomas checked the horizon in every square, glaring at the growing dust cloud beyond the town that may or may not have been Marwin. *Damn this and damn her too!* Elisabeth was closing in and the wind was rising as the sun began to set. *Williams' hound is going to earn her keep if we don't hurry.*

Back at the fountain with the keyhole, he hurled a piece of stone through the empty window of a nearby house. It hit the far wall with a muted clack. "We don't even know if this wild goose chase is worth the trouble."

"Would you rather run? We've probably wasted too much time already, I don't think we have a choice now."

He sighed, letting his shoulders slump. She was right. "Well, we could try breaking it."

"Do we have a sledgehammer?"

"I have a regular hammer; took it from the jeep, remember?"

"And do you really want to break the fountain?"

"No. But it feels like..." Thomas shook his head; he was a fool. He'd overlooked an obvious possibility. "The chest in the room beside the staircase." It wasn't a guarantee – of anything – but it was worth a look.

He led Mia back to the inn and then into the dim room. "It's the only thing in the building that was hidden behind two locks. Water is precious. It stands to reason that something else valuable, something useful, is here."

"Let's see."

He hooked the claw of his hammer into the lock and brought his hand down hard on the handle. A snap followed and the padlock clattered to the floor. He frowned. Even with his usual strength, it had been easier than he'd expected. *Must have been weakened.* He set the hammer aside and placed a hand on the latch. "Ready?"

"This isn't a magic trick, Thomas, no need to check on the audience."

He grinned to himself as he lifted the lid.

Within lay a small stack of L-shaped handles with elaborately-decorated hand grips of silver filigree. He lifted one free; the shaft was fitted with evenly-spaced square protrusions like teeth on a key. It also bore a carved image, an hourglass with a keyhole in the sand. "Take this." He handed the key to Mia, unable to keep a feathery trace of hope from his voice. If it worked, they'd have access to enough water to give them a real chance... supposing there was another town within reach.

And supposing Elisabeth didn't catch them first.

Suddenly his hope faltered a little.

Mia ran her hands over the teeth. "This is a perfect fit. Why did they hide these?" she asked. "Why close the fountains?"

"Perhaps the river ran dry."

"Or they did it to protect the water from whoever drove them from their homes." She tossed the handle back. "Come on."

Back at the fountain, key in hand, he paused as another dark thought rose. What if the fountains had been sealed not to protect the town's water from some threat, but to protect the town from the water? "What if it's poisonous?"

Mia frowned. "I hadn't thought of that."

"Maybe I shouldn't have said it. We're still running out of options."

"Give it a shot then."

He inserted the key, lining up the teeth with the holes and it slid in with a satisfying clink. Then he took a breath and gripped the handle, putting pressure on. It did not move. He tried again, arm straining. *Two hands then.* Thomas added more pressure to the handle, feeling the blood rush to his face as it turned red. "Come on," he growled.

The sound of grinding stone followed. *Finally!*

Once it started, the winding became easier. He worked the lever like an oarsman, turning it over and over until the grinding of stone stopped and the handle would move no more.

No water spurted free.

The sculpture remained still, features darkening in the failing light. But from the other side of the fountain a puff of dust rose. He took a few paces and stopped. "Mia."

The very earth beside the fountain's wall had opened, revealing steps leading down into shadow. Mia joined him, a hand brushing against his shoulder – the low light was obviously stealing what little vision she'd been given.

"The ground was vibrating while you worked," she said. "I can't hear the water."

"I don't know if it's really a fountain. There's an underground passage."

"This is what we were meant to discover," Mia replied, her tone certain.

"A place to hide from Elisabeth?"

"Why not? The hog will be here in an hour or two, won't it?"

"Less."

"There's no-where else to hide. And I don't like our chances running through the night."

He pointed to the fountain, though she'd only sense the movement. "How do we close the thing?"

"Check inside," Mia said.

He took his own rifle from where he'd leant it against his pack and the dwindling water barrel. Pointing the weapon into the darkness as he climbed down, no figure leapt forth, no sounds resonated from below. In the poor light he gave up using his eyes, instead feeling around the walls for an opening. His fingertips and palms slid over rough stone until... there. A regular opening, large enough for him to reach inside and find the holes for the key.

"This might just work," he called up.

Mia appeared above him, a darker shadow against an indigo sky. "What about light?"

"Hold on." He returned to remove a heavy lantern from his pack, winding the cogs before raising the light, letting the warm glow fill the space. Smooth steps led the way down into the earth, the brickwork on the stair and the walls impressively neat.

"Feel the wall," he said softly.

Mia ran a hand across the carefully fitted stone. "This is so... exact. Who would build such a tunnel?"

"And why?"

"Do you think..." Mia trailed off, lifting her hand from the wall.

Thomas opened his mouth to ask what was wrong but a vibration in the very earth stopped him. Faint yet, it grew in intensity the longer he listened. *A constant reminder.* "The sand-hog."

"This is probably our last chance to run," Mia said.

"I know." Still he did not move, he only gripped the handle in his free hand, running a thumb across the silver scrollwork.

"Thomas?"

"Can you feel anything... I don't know, evil down there?"

"I feel nothing."

"All right." Her gift had served them truly so far. *But will it stay that way?* He didn't really have a reason to doubt, especially since Mia seemed to have accepted her gift. *She trusts it, I should too.* He took their water, slipped his pack over his shoulder, fitted the key to the lock and began turning.

Chapter 6

Hours had passed and while the rumbling from Elisabeth's war machine had fallen away after a lull, as they'd no doubt searched the town, Thomas' relief was dampened by the dwindling lantern oil. Its glow still illuminated the brick tunnel, which had descended and evened out to level ground for long stretches, turning but once, early on. At his best estimation, they were heading east again.

But to where?

Only the damp, muted echo of their boots filled the tunnel.

Time stretched on. Was it midnight yet? No way to be sure, but his legs were growing tired, so a few hours at least had probably passed. The pack wasn't getting any lighter either. *Like a sack full of bloody granite.* But there was no way he was jettisoning the last of their water.

When a wide chamber finally appeared before them he slowed. Mia touched his arm. "A room," he said.

"Empty?"

He raised the lantern higher. At the far end was

something that looked like a mining cart, only more solid. The wheels were heavier and the sides of the cart high; it even bore a set of steps leading up. "No, there's a cart, but I don't know if it's for mining."

He climbed the steps and peered over the edge. Twin bench seats faced each other, fashioned in aged leather. Affixed to what he assumed was the rear of the cart was a large box bearing a circular opening. The same pattern and hourglass-with-keyhole symbol they'd found on the fountain ringed it. *Who would use the slave's mark like that? Has the Williams dynasty been here?* When he'd asked Mia upon finding the first symbol, she'd been doubtful.

"What kind of cart?" Mia asked. "I don't feel any change in the air – where does it go? Back the way we came?"

Where did the cart go indeed? Tracks led directly to a blank, featureless wall but there was no indication of how it could be opened, or even if it *did* open. But surely the handle would operate the cart somehow. "Through the wall I think," he replied. "There's another key hole in the cart. Let's try it."

Once he'd helped Mia in and set the lantern down, he sat on the cold bench seat across from the box to slot the key within. It clicked into place and he turned the handle, testing the resistance. Before him, stone began to rasp across stone as the wall slid across an inch. How was the cart connected to the wall? "There is a way forward," Thomas said.

He continued to turn the handle, the wall sliding open until a stygian passage appeared before them. Was there the faintest sense of movement in the air now? Or, was it simply wishful thinking? There was the sense of a great age, great mystery to the entire tunnel and the town above... but it was a mystery that could be solved later. *After we find more water. And after we see if this tunnel even leads anywhere.*

Elisabeth remained an unseen, uncertain threat. But threat she still was. The empty town might have thrown her off only temporarily for all he knew. And her giant air canons would certainly reduce the homes and fountains to rubble if she wanted to search again. *Now you're being paranoid. She has no reason to suspect the fountains lead to anything.* He frowned at the handle in his grip. *Unless she returns and searches the inn and finds the chest – she'll put it together.*

"Thomas, what's wrong?"

"Just thinking about Elisabeth. She won't search the desert around the town forever. She'll go back, look harder. Once she figures out the fountain, she'll be on our trail again."

"Assuming she does. And assuming she chooses the same fountain," Mia said.

"Maybe so, but I don't even know if this tunnel is taking us anywhere."

"We have to keep going," she said, her voice full of a calm he found himself envying.

"I know." He started turning the handle again, and slowly, awfully slowly, the passenger cart started forward, wheels squeaking from disuse. Mia settled herself into the seat as he worked. The cart gained enough momentum to pass into the passage. He glanced up from his work – the lantern light revealed rough-hewn walls and roof. But when he paused to glance over the side, the rail ran along a smooth surface, big wheels deep in the track. Solid. *This thing would be hard to shake off the track.*

During his assessment the cart had slowed; he grunted

as he worked double-time to get it moving again. He was soon sweating but the cart continued to pick up speed. Yet the work was not impossible. His body could handle it, almost as if he had an affinity for working with steel. *Or maybe it's just an affinity for labour.* He paused when a gentle slope appeared ahead. Just how fast was this thing going to travel? If the tunnel grew steep... He eased off on the handle then slumped into the seat.

"What's ahead?" Mia asked.

"Just darkness. The tunnel will slope down soon."

"Just tell me if I need to duck," Mia said as she took hold of the sides.

The passenger cart started down the slope and their passage quickened. The stone in the walls began to roll by, lantern light soon barely having enough time to touch it. The tunnel swept down yet further.

Thomas held the sides but the vessel flew true, not even a hint of a wobble or bump in the path. How long would the ride last? And where would it end? At a sudden wall, with their mangled corpses? Did he have to wind the handle the opposite direction to slow the cart?

The lantern fluttered and died.

Thomas gripped the edge of the cart a little harder. The passage of air across his face was chill in the surrounding blackness; the flight of the cart suddenly became wild, reckless.

And yet – if he took a moment to breathe, it was smooth as ever.

Powerless.

He sneered at himself. *Isn't this what Mia faces every day? Get a grip.*

"What's wrong?" Mia asked.

"The lantern died," he said.

"I noticed." A moment of silence. "Don't be afraid, Thomas."

"It's hard not to be – what if we're hurtling toward a wall?" The degree of the slope, while not too sharp, made the vague possibility of slowing the cart with the handle seem impossible.

"I don't believe that – we're on the right path, I can tell." Conviction was clear in her voice.

She'd been right before. It was enough to take the edge off his discomfort as their simple carriage flew through the shadow, heading ever-downward.

Time in the darkness stretched on.

He couldn't judge how long and he rarely spoke with Mia; the tension of their flight and search took its toll and he dozed. Each time, he jerked awake – certain they were moments from thundering into an unseen obstacle.

Yet when the tunnel evened out and the cart began to slow, he straightened from where he'd slumped against the soft leather. Had he fallen asleep again? "Mia?"

"It's all right," she said. "We're still safe. I never felt any danger."

He peered ahead. Was that a grey smudge in the distance, still small? The patch of light grew bigger and bigger until he was certain. An opening! "There's a way out," he said.

"How close?"

"Not long at all."

The cart had already gained enough distance that the opening was at least twice as wide enough for their vehicle and more than three times as tall, there was even a hint of a warm breeze blowing into the tunnel. The smoky-steel glow was that of a growing dawn. The carriage slowed further until it thumped against a solid stockade, lining up with another cart, both shapes little more than vague shadows as he squinted at the new light. Here, where the tunnel opened into a large cave, light poured within.

Mia was already climbing free and heading toward the light. "Can you hear that?"

Thomas gathered the lantern and his pack before leaping after her. The cavern stood wide and empty but a heavy steel rail lined its edge. There was a small gate barring access to a broad, long walkway – and the soft roar seemed to rest beyond it. What could it be?

His steps faltered when he joined Mia at the rail.

Far below, an ocean stretched forth – stretched further than his eye could fathom, its deep blue smouldering with secrets. Thomas could not compare its majesty to anything else. Molten ripples seemed to cover restless creatures, slow-moving but still dangerous, the *endlessness* of it stole away his words.

Not even the bright shores of the Royal Lake could rival the ocean – and few slaves had ever seen the Lake at that, let alone an ocean.

"What is it?" Mia asked, her voice soft in the hush. "It feels so vast."

"The Northern Ocean." He took her hand, a stone sinking in his chest. *She deserves to see this*. "I wish I could describe it to you but I'd only get it wrong."

"Try," she said, giving his hand a squeeze.

Chapter 7

The steel walkway beyond the gate extended from the rock face, supported by impressive steel arches the like of which he had never seen before, not even in the smog-choked capital with its mechanical wonders. Just who had made such a structure? And what was it for? Why would someone walk out such a distance so high above an ocean?

"It's for an airship." Mia stood above him, leaning on the rail. "This is where it would dock. Maybe supply the town above."

He looked up from where he lay on the grated steel, no longer peering over the side to the dark rock face. Bolts twice the size of his chest had been driven into the mountain to help affix the supports. "I hadn't thought of that."

She shrugged. "If this place is as old as you say... why not?"

"No-one's seen an airship for seventy years at least."

"True."

An airship. Thomas shook his head. *Forget it.* That dream was finished – no-one escaped their dying continent. Even ex-slaves would one day die in the arid wastes or the grime-caked cities. He lifted himself into a sitting position, staring down toward the water where a second walkway jutted from the mountain. It lay much closer to the ocean's surface, accessible from above via a narrow stone stair that hugged the cliff-face. It would be a long walk – half the day at least.

Yet it was their destination nonetheless.

While such structures hardly guaranteed the presence of people, of water or food, it had to be explored. The sun was already climbing too, which would mean an unpleasant trek down. Although, perhaps the ocean would lessen the harshness once they neared it.

He drew his flask free and took a sip. Their water would last a day longer yet. "Let's see what's down there."

The path was narrow but not perilously so. Mia kept one hand trailing the rock wall as she walked and he glanced back, checking on her often but she placed each foot confidently, her willow rifle in her other hand. It brushed each step so she could gauge the height – not all steps were even.

Halfway down, those who'd carved the steps had taken the time to hollow out part of the mountain to create a wide landing. A spot to rest, perhaps, or somewhere for those with heavy loads to pass one another. *Either way, it's still nice to take a moment.* He went and sat against the wall, shading his face from the sun.

Mia drank from her own flask before joining him. "I want to try something." She closed her eyes and began to hum, the same lullaby from the dim reaches of their childhood, the same tune that she had the mechanical birds singing, the same song that had brought the great bird of fire down to save them back at the *Esmeralda*. He almost expected the bird to appear again, streaking across the ocean toward them but nothing happened.

"Maybe we need to be in danger for it to work," Mia said with a shrug when she finished.

They soon resumed their descent.

Thomas' leg muscles ached, his back too, especially burdened as he was. But as he neared the end of the stair, sweat dripping from his hair, it seemed there would be a reward. A whisper of smoke appeared from beyond an outcropping, scattered by the wondrous, cool breeze that slipped up off the waves that were now topped by glittering white peaks.

"Someone lives nearby," Thomas said as they passed the gate to the second docking point. Only a little ways further and they'd reach a broad path close to sea-level, the source of the smoke obscured by a large rock wall. It was natural up to a point; nearest the path it became half an arch of brickwork. Unfinished, or by design?

Thomas tapped Mia on the shoulder as they passed it and she edged a little closer as they did.

A stone village clung to the mountain and extended out into the very ocean. Waves lapped against solid foundations – not unlike stilts used by performers in the circus he'd once snuck into. The sea had done little to erode the mighty stone pillars; salt stained, they did not seem in danger of collapsing or of tipping the homes they supported into the deep blue water.

Each building sat like a square block with a peaked roof of slate, probably harvested from the shores if the jagged beach was any indication. Pink and green vines climbed around the windows of most homes and the hint of smoke he'd seen earlier came from several buildings, though no-one walked the rocky paths.

"It's a paradise," he said softly, explaining the vista to Mia.

"Let's hope there's a welcoming party then," she said. "And not more of Williams' men."

"Either way, we need water," he replied. But she was right. If more soldiers lurked among the peaceful-seeming homes there would be few options open to them. Flee into the ocean or surrender, probably. *You can't take on an entire town with two rifles.*

"I feel no danger, if that helps."

"Then we'll try the nearest home." Thomas started up the path, eyes roving for any sign of trouble, Mia following a little slower. When he knocked on the door no-one answered. He stood back from the eaves and glanced at the roof – it wasn't one of the homes with smoke rising from the stone chimney.

He tried the next house, and this time a woman in a shapeless smock opened the door, the beginning of a smile on her face – as if expecting a neighbour perhaps – only for the expression to disappear. Her skin was as tanned as any on the continent, but her hair was fairer than Thomas had come to expect and her grey eyes were unlike any others.

"I'm sorry to startle you," he said. "But we're travellers seeking aid."

She frowned at him but did not answer. Had she understood his words? Thomas tried again, this time speaking a little slower. "Can you help us?"

The woman said something that sounded like 'mustal' before smiling at them both, though it faltered a little when she noticed Mia's blindfold. The woman still waved them back into the street where she beckoned for them to follow. Maybe their luck would hold yet – the woman didn't seem duplicitous. Thomas guided Mia over the wandering paths to one of the large, three-storey homes that held a small balcony. A white bird with orange feet stood regarding them as their guide rang a bell on a chain.

An old man eventually opened the door – his own pale eyes widening at the sight of Thomas and Mia. The woman and he exchanged a few words before she left, smiling once more at Thomas.

"Please come inside," the old man said, running a gnarled hand over his bald head. His speech was clear but an odd emphasis lay across the words, as if he were concentrating hard to recall them.

"Thank you," Thomas said.

The old timer took them to armchairs that had been arranged before a hearth of embers. A pot steamed silently above the heat. "Can I offer you tea, travellers?"

Thomas shook his head but Mia answered in the affirmative.

"Do folk from above still take it with lemon?"

Thomas looked to Mia, whose mouth had fallen open as she turned to face his direction. "You have lemon?"

He wheezed a laugh. "Of course, we get it from the Twilight Islands across the sea."

"We haven't seen a lemon in years," Mia said.

"Well, I'll fix you some with your tea while we talk," he said as he stood, heading for another room. The ease of his speech was improving the longer he spoke. He returned after but a moment, a plump-looking lemon in hand. When he reached for a knife on the sill above the fireplace, Thomas caught sight of a faded tattoo on his wrist.

A red hourglass.

First among slaves. Honoured above others, honoured with responsibility – yet caged by virtue of whatever skill the Kings needed. A rare sight indeed. *But not so different to the yellow; we're all slaves in the end.*

"My name is Henry," he said as he cut lemon slices, squeezing a little into each of the three cups he'd brought with him. "I'm something of a village elder, I guess. Or maybe more like a mayor. Do you still have mayors up there or has old man Williams done away with them too?" His voice had taken on a harder edge.

"Most towns are run by puppets or the military," Thomas said after introducing himself and his sister. "I take it from your tattoo that you're referring to the current Williams' late father?"

"I am," he said. "And I'd spit too, but not with a lady present."

Mia smiled. "I'd join you."

Henry laughed again. "Well, you must be curious about this place – and I admit, I'd like to know how you found us."

Thomas rummaged within his pack a moment, withdrawing the ornate handle. "We found an empty town in our flight across the desert."

"And we must warn you, we're being pursued by Williams' men," Mia added. "We closed the way but if they discover what we did... I would hate to bring trouble here."

Henry lowered his cup. "How many?"

"Perhaps dozens, we can't be certain," she said. "They will be well-armed."

He sighed. "We have had peace for a long time – it was

never promised to last forever. But I feel for the young ones, who haven't had as much time as I, and who would not survive slavery."

"You did. And we have," Thomas said.

"For now, yes," Henry replied. He squinted at Thomas' forearm. "Your tattoo – the hourglass is yellow, isn't it?"

Thomas pushed his sleeve higher, revealing the slave's mark.

Henry nodded. "So, you were once slaves to the so-called aristocracy?" He sighed as he settled in his chair. "In some ways an easier life than those who toil in mines or factories under the weight of the black or white hourglass. But would you claim that you craved freedom any less than those men and women?"

"No," Thomas said. And some of those with the white or black might have argued that slaves like Thomas and Henry *did* have freedom, the freedom at least to have been stationed above their labouring counterparts. At the very least, the word of a palace slave in the Fortress tended to fare better than the word of a factory-man, that much Thomas would have conceded.

But never being able to make his own decisions… that was not freedom.

Mia shook her head, her jaw set.

"And so it will be with the people here," Henry said.

"Does your tattoo count for nothing now?" Thomas asked. "We have only ever met one other bearing a red hourglass."

"Maybe I'm one of the last. I was a gifted blacksmith once… valuable to the 'king', I suppose…" he trailed off with a shrug. "But the details of my mistakes aren't important. I made them and it landed me such a mark. It wasn't until years later that I learnt of this place and escaped, and that's a whole other crime, isn't it? I could barter for nothing, lad."

"Someone else here, perhaps?"

"No. A now scattered, forgotten resistance group concocted the escape of those who fled into the desert and built the town you saw – even with help there was a mighty cost. Generations later and most here have never known the bite of a needle and ink in their skin – I fear for these people now."

"Then we will leave," Thomas said. "Draw Elisabeth and her men away if they come."

Henry offered a sad smile. "Unless you have an airship in that pack of yours, leave is something you cannot do, for there is only one path leading from Silver Rock and that's the way you came in."

Chapter 8

Thomas paced a beach of jumbled stone, the ocean breeze stirring his hair. He stopped, his arms folded as he stared across the endless swathe of water. He still hadn't come up with any ideas but at least it was cool on the shore.

Mia stood nearby and Henry sat on a flat rock behind her; its grey surface perhaps too dull for the town's romantic name. The old timer chuckled. "The ship won't arrive just because you're watching, lad."

"Would they take us all on even if it did?" he asked.

"Well, we'd certainly fit."

The 'ship' was the *Albion*, an iron relic that still traded between other nations but also, it seemed, Brasatalis – even now, decades after the old bans that isolated their country from most of the rest of the world. Thomas had never seen the ship, but supposedly David, their protector, had. "It was so enormous, Tom... like an iron city floating in the water. The stacks were like pillars reaching up to heaven – or, spewing steam up there anyway," he had said. The *Albion* once regularly brought rare goods, certain medicines and luxuries but Williams' grandfather had put a stop to all that with his refusal to sign the anti-slavery treaty with the other nations. *And what a dying waste our land is becoming now.* "You said it was due to visit, didn't you?" Thomas asked Henry.

"I did. This is her season but there's no way to tell exactly which day. Could be two more, could be ten or twenty." He glanced across the waves. "There's no guarantee either. Some years the *Albion* doesn't come at all, and it's not like her captain sends word. He's breaking the treaty by trading with us."

"What do you offer him?" Mia asked.

Henry turned to her. "I can show you, if you like? It's something you can hold," he added.

"Yes, please. I could use the distraction," Mia said. "Thomas?"

"Why not? I'm not coming up with anything here."

"Then follow me," Henry said.

Henry led them through the town, waving to the occasional man or woman working in small gardens. Everyone waved back, curiosity or fear in their gaze, but no-one approached. Beyond the row of homes, still hugging the coast, waited a path with familiar, deep-set rails.

"Who built this?" Thomas asked as they approached a large opening in the wall of stone.

"The resistance group I mentioned. Many years ago," Henry said. "Gatehouse. They were clever but too few. They built the airship landings too; you would have passed them on your way down."

"What happened?" Mia asked.

He paused at the mouth of the cavern. "I don't know, truly. Some say they were betrayed by one of their own, others that the Williams' dynasty simply overwhelmed them with numbers." He moved deeper into the cave and not very far in, stepped beside a cart. This was like the passenger cart, in that it had the same design and box but it was smaller. A heavy pick-axe leaned against it and the suggestion of braced arches was visible just beyond the limit of the light.

A mine.

Henry gestured them closer. "This is what we trade."

Thomas approached and let out a gasp. The cart was full of precious stones, their glittering muted but the clarity and size of the pieces was like nothing he'd ever seen, not even on the jewellery of the ladies of the Fortress. "Can I touch one?" Thomas asked.

"Of course."

Thomas lifted a piece of diamond so it caught more of the light from the opening, setting it afire with colour, despite a cloudy patch. Henry had already handed a fist-sized ruby to Mia, who ran her fingertips over the surface. "Jewels?" she asked. "This is so heavy."

"If Williams found this..." Thomas said.

"It probably wouldn't matter," Henry replied. "Williams doesn't have the tools or, more importantly, the expertise to create fine work from uncut gemstones. Few do actually."

"Nor the trade agreements," Thomas said, nodding to himself.

"So where do they go?" Mia asked.

"The *Albion* takes them to Europa. They're the only ones who can refine the stones. Then they sell to the rest of the world – excluding our so-called aristocracy. *They* cling to heirlooms only."

Thomas replaced the jewel. "This is still a secret that you

must keep, surely."

"Perhaps," he said. "But we have no visitors – you are the first since I have been here and the *Albion* comes only once a season, bringing much-needed goods. We have little else to offer."

"What could we barter for passage?" Mia asked.

Henry hesitated and Thomas gripped the side of the cart. The iron ship was an opportunity like no other. Freedom, true freedom – a way to escape Williams *and* the dying land. "Do you think the Captain would take us? I can work and Mia—"

He shook his head slowly but there was compassion in his eyes. No doubt, as an ex-slave, Henry understood their desperation only too well. "Captain Hawkins has always refused passengers; I don't believe he would risk smuggling anyone into another nation. Especially not someone from our land."

Thomas let his shoulders slump; hope dying before he let it take hold. "Then we will find a way to run again."

Mia put a hand on his arm. "There was never a guarantee the *Albion* would beat Elisabeth anyway."

"That's not very comforting, sis," he said.

"I know, but maybe we can reach the Twilight Islands," Mia turned her blindfolded face to the silhouette of Henry. "Can we make a raft, somehow?"

Henry scratched at his head. "There was once an old forest along the coast. Two days travel but it might be worth a look, *if* the trees have survived."

"Then that's what we will try," she said, with a determined nod.

"After we make sure Elisabeth cannot come here,"

Thomas added.

"How?" Mia asked.

"I don't know. Could we collapse the tunnel somehow?"

Mia frowned. "I don't see how."

Henry chuckled. "Slow down, you two. You don't have to collapse it; the tunnel can be closed. I've not seen it done, but everything else Gatehouse made still works. Follow me again."

Chapter 9

Henry stood with his hands on his hips before the heavy-steel door set in the mountain, breathing hard. Thomas didn't blame him; it had been a long climb back up, even bolstered by a meal of fish and greens. The slowly setting sun was turning the water gold and the temperature was already starting to drop.

"In there," Henry said, waving a key at the door. His key was much more conventional in size and shape compared to the one Thomas had found above. Henry nodded to a pair of the villagers who'd accompanied them, and the young men ran into the tunnel. Their faces were stern and they carried with them some sort of bronze cone with a dial, which, presumably, could be used to hear if anyone was in the tunnel. *More wondrous machinery left behind by Gatehouse, no doubt.*

After a bit of jiggling and muttering beneath his breath, Henry had the door unlocked. It squeaked open. "We don't use this room much, since no-one's ever been able to make the machines work. Besides which, we still head into the desert sometimes."

"To check on the old town?" Mia asked.

Henry shook his head. "For snake venom. We use it in our medicine."

Thomas guided Mia into the room behind Henry, though she probably didn't need the help. But she didn't complain at his solicitousness, she never did. *It's more patience than I'd have.*

Within, he described what he saw. Two walls covered in steel panels, huge rivets driven into the stone. The same walls bore a series of levers, dozens of them, usually in pairs, each marked with rigid symbols. *Old numbers?* A secret series of symbols used only by Gatehouse? When he neared the panels, a faint tingling crossed his skin, so gentle that he wondered if he hadn't imagined it. The third wall was more of a steel mesh with a gate, silent, motionless cogs visible beyond. Some were huge, spanning nearly the entire wall, and others the size of his knuckle. *Delicate work.*

Henry was stretching up to a shelf that appeared to have been installed after the main construction. He lifted down a leather-bound book, one of several, its edges capped in tarnished copper. "This is all we have left from them. From Gatehouse."

Thomas accepted the book but did not open it at once. Instead, he looked to the levers. "You think it's one of these?"

"Yes, but none work. They move, but nothing happens. And as far as I can tell, the machinery is sound." He frowned at the wall with the cogs and chains.

Mia moved to the levers, a hand outstretched. "Let me... there's something here, with time perhaps..."

"We have time," Henry said. "The brothers will warn us if

anyone approaches via the tunnel."

Thomas lifted the book and leant against the wall beside the entryway and Henry joined him as he opened the first page. It revealed a pair of crossed forearms, their hourglass tattoos had been modified – each now included a keyhole in the sand. *Like on the handle.* On the second page, a sepia photograph of a young man with a shock of dark hair, grinning as he worked on a huge engine, spanner in hand and goggles around his neck.

Written beneath the image was a date – nearly one hundred years ago.

"That's Jean," Henry said. "The best pilot the Gatehouse had."

"He's young."

"Around twenty at the time, I'd say."

The next photo was obviously taken from the cavern just outside, it showed the walkway bustling with people in vests or open shirts, women in tights and boots, many of them armed with rifles. The figure nearest the camera had a revolver belted at her waist but Thomas noted the detail absently; his eyes were drawn to the magnificent airship docked at the end of the walkway.

Its sleek body was armoured and about half the porthole windows were open, canons resting beneath them. Gatling guns lined the bridge and aft and fore, near a headpiece shaped as a woman with wings. Men clung to the rigging beneath the balloon, a grey or perhaps even tan, Thomas couldn't be sure. A giant keyhole had been painted on its side, along with a slogan in archaic script, difficult to read due to the angle of the photograph.

The propellers and engine were not visible but he wished

they were – the airship filled him with a sense of awe and even a sliver of desperation. Something he'd tried to squash many times before, but seeing the picture brought all the childhood dreams rushing back. *I'm a fool. It's a child's dream, nothing more.*

"What happened to the airship?" Thomas asked.

Henry sighed. "No-one knows for sure; it is said to have disappeared in the southern wastes of Viterra."

"Then it might still be there? The royal family never found it?"

"If they had, they'd be flying it around, you can be sure of that."

Thomas nodded as he flipped through the other pages. There were more images of Jean, sometimes alone, sometimes surrounded by an assortment of men and women, some men bearded, some – men and women both – with close-shaven heads, others clothed in bowler hats not unlike those worn by the aristocracy. All armed heavily. Not many images revealed smiles like the first; it seemed a serious group. *And why shouldn't they be? Defying the Dirt Kings. Daring to be free.* Other pages bore more text, none of which he could read. Others still were sketches of mechanical parts, not all of it seeming to be steam-powered and none of which made much sense.

"Who collected all of this?" he asked.

"Check the end and then flip back to the picture with everyone raising a toast on the beach."

At the back page rested a name and a date in the same handwriting as the rest of the book, dated several years after the first image. "Stella Blackmoor." He switched to the image, happy faces around a huge fire on a beach. Each lifted a mug or glass. Beneath, a tiny note: *Celebrating victory of our first aerial battle.*

"Stella is across from Jean, holding the T-square."

She was beautiful; her eyes luminous in triumph, even with her head shaven so close that her hair was little more than the suggestion of a shadow. Her hourglass tattoo was visible where she'd raised her glass, was it yellow or red? Impossible to tell but he doubted it had been white or black.

Approaching footsteps echoed up the tunnel.

Thomas lowered the book and Henry looked to the door and Mia too, turned from her examination of the levers.

The brothers appeared and approached Henry, apprehension clear in their voices as they spoke. One gestured back toward the tunnel and Henry's expression grew grim. He sent the men back to the town, and they set off at a run. His voice was quiet when he spoke. "The boys heard the tread of many boots in the tunnel and the grinding of wheels."

"How close?" Mia asked, her voice tight.

"Less than an hour."

"That should be enough time – I know how to restore the levers," she said.

"Truly?" Henry's demeanour lifted.

She reached for the largest two levers. "As you've probably guessed, these two operate the doors on the cavern mouth. If you can restart the boiler, we should be able to close the doors. I just have to get the sequence right in here."

Henry used his key on the gate that prevented access to the cog room. "My predecessor had been left no instructions, how will you know?" he asked Mia.

"I can't really explain it," she said. "But I can almost sense the right order."

Henry frowned.

"She led us here," Thomas said.

The old man gave a short nod and waved his hand. "All right."

Thomas glanced to Mia. "Will you be fine here?"

"Just tell me when you restart it."

He hesitated a moment longer. Henry had already started along the walkway but Thomas had to listen. Could he hear the muffled, still-distant tread of boots, or was it only his fear?

"Thomas, I'll call if I hear anything. The engine room isn't so large," she said. "I've seen it all in my mind, go. Quickly."

"All right." He entered the engine room, chasing after Henry, lantern swinging in his hand. The giant cogs towered above him, the steel gleaming in the light. Chains ran high above and deep below, disappearing into the mountain. Each link had to have been as tall as he himself. Smaller cogs were all as well-kept as the rest of the control room.

Thomas followed the walkway around a corner and found Henry standing before a huge boiler. The furnace hatch lay open, cold. Beside the boiler rested a broad copper pipe with a circular handle. The pipe extended down beneath the walkway, disappearing into the dark depths far below.

Henry straightened from where he was examining a dial. "We need to get this started quickly; I don't know how long it will take to get hot enough."

A squat door rested beside the furnace. Within, Thomas found a wide-mouthed shovel and a bellows with copper grips, each lying within a bed of coal. "How about I take the first shift, Henry?"

Henry nodded and Thomas shovelled some coal in, smashing a few pieces almost to dust with the side of the shovel, then the old man took the lantern and covered the coal with oil. Then he added a burning wick to the bed. The flames were slow to catch. "Without a proper base, this might not work at all," Henry said, fanning it with the bellows.

Heat was slow to build.

Mia's voice echoed from the other room. "They're getting closer."

"Where's the water?" Thomas asked.

"Maybe this." Henry strode to the copper pipe, grasping the handle. He strained, but the wheel did not budge. He tried again, veins in his wrists starting to bulge. "It might as well be frozen," he finally said.

"Let's switch." Thomas handed the shovel over and took the handle, straining against the wheel. Nothing. Not even the hint of movement. He leant into the task, bracing his legs, grunting with the effort until it finally started to screech its way open. He kept the pressure on and a warmth seemed to build in his muscles, knuckles whitening as the handle spun all the way open. Then he leant back against the wall to catch his breath, the heat in his limbs fading. He'd pushed himself too far, it seemed.

The sound of rushing water, deep, became audible. Thomas straightened. "It's working. How are the flames?"

"The fire's holding on." Henry dashed back to the hatch.

Thomas checked the boiler's dial. A marker stood at one hundred degrees Celsius but the needle was barely creeping up toward five. "I'm checking on Mia," he said.

Henry only nodded, carefully shovelling more coal.

In the control room, Mia still stood by the main levers, her head tilted to the sound of echoing boots. Thomas stepped to the doorway, glancing into the tunnel. Nothing but darkness, no sign of Elisabeth yet. But how long would that last?

"I have the sequence; it's ready. Is the boiler working?" Mia asked.

Thomas didn't turn from the tunnel. "It's starting from cold; I don't know."

"Maybe I can help," she said. "When you hear my call, pull these two."

"What?"

"Trust me," she said, and started for the boiler room, trailing one hand along the wall, already starting to hum the old lullaby. Thomas caught his breath. *Does she mean....* "Mia, not the Bird of Light? How do you know it will work?"

"I don't know," she called back.

Thomas shook his head but the heavy tread of boots echoing stopped him answering. *Maybe it's worth a shot.*

Chapter 10

In the boiler room Mia lifted her voice but Thomas couldn't tear his eyes from the tunnel – was that a hint of movement beyond the very limits of light? The thunder of footfalls grew louder, joined by voices.

He glanced over his shoulder.

Light blazed from the boiler room. Henry's voice echoed; a cry of shock. *She did it again!* But would there be enough heat? Was it a bird of fire and light, or only light? It hadn't seemed to be both back at the wreck of the *Esmeralda*.

"Look," a voice cried from the tunnel.

Thomas spun back to the darkness. Shapes *were* visible now. A tall figure resolved from the shadows, indistinct yet, but by the build it had to be Elisabeth.

"Now, Thomas!" Mia shouted.

He ran, diving for the levers. His hand wrapped around steel and he ripped them downward. Somewhere within the mountain a rumbling followed, a deep groaning as if something woke from a long slumber.

Shouts of alarm rose from the tunnel. He snatched a rifle

and leapt into the cavern. High above, a mighty gate was sliding down from the roof. It had to have been half as thick as it was wide – a monster. Dust fell with it and while the pace was steady, the charging figures were closing the gap swiftly. Thomas went to one knee as he raised the rifle and fired.

One of the shapes fell. Dead or wounded, he could not tell.

The front line faltered but kept on, soldiers raising their own weapons. The tallest figure, Elisabeth – he could see her flowing hair now – did not stop, she only ran harder. The wall was well over halfway closed now.

"This won't stop us forever, Thomas," Elisabeth shouted.

Bullets pinged against the wall and Thomas fell back, no longer able to take any more shots himself. Elisabeth snarled a curse, her voice cut off as the door boomed shut. The very cavern seemed to shake, though it could have been the ringing in his ears. Thomas slumped against the gate and exhaled heavily, closing his eyes.

Safe.

He could hear the faintest sound of impotent fury from beyond but not even Elisabeth's steam-canons could break through such a door. She'd be forced to try something else, and whatever it was, there was a chance the *Albion* would have come and gone by then.

Footsteps rushed toward him. He looked up – only Henry, with Mia not far behind. The old timer was grinning and even Mia wore a smile. "It worked, didn't it," she said.

"Thanks to you."

"I can hardly believe it myself," Henry said, awe within his voice. "And I saw the bird with my own eyes, *through* them. It's nothing short of a miracle."

Mia swallowed, her tone uncertain. "I'm not sure about that."

Henry placed a hand on the mighty gate, continuing as if he had not heard her. "And this is as solid as the very mountain itself, you've doubtless saved us."

"We should probably still post a watch," Thomas said. "Just to be sure."

"We will."

Darkness had now fallen across the sea and the lone remaining lamp cast only enough light to create a pool around them. *Time to make a start back down.* He hoped the oil would last the long descent back to the village of Silver Rock. Henry was confident when Thomas asked, leading them down. "More than enough, lad."

By the landing, Thomas had to knuckle his eyes when they paused. How long now since they'd had a decent night's sleep? Mia was quiet and even Henry's earlier jubilance had faded. When they finally entered the village, deep into the night, it was with only mumbled words that he thanked Henry, who had directed them to an empty home that consisted of a single large room with two beds and a stove. Thomas knelt by the fireplace to light the dried seaweed while Mia thanked the man.

"I'll send Sarasi with breakfast at dawn," Henry said at the door.

"Only if it's not too much trouble," Mia said.

"No trouble at all. Sleep well."

The door closed as Thomas stumbled toward one of the beds, little more than a net strung across a frame. No blankets, but he didn't care. The room would warm soon enough and even the acrid scent of burning seaweed wouldn't stop him falling asleep.

"Thomas?" The sounds of Mia dumping her pack and settling into the second bed – hammock, really – were loud in the hush.

"Huh?"

"What do you think it means?"

Thomas turned to face her. She lay in the bed, her blindfold removed and her face troubled in the flickering firelight. He shook off some of his sleepiness. "The bird?"

"Yes. And the... predictions or feelings or whatever they are. Why is it happening to me?"

"I don't know," he said softly. "But I don't think it's a bad thing, at least. Do you?"

"Maybe. It's obviously why Williams is chasing us."

He sighed as he stared up at the shadows of the ceiling. "It might be the very thing that saves us from him too."

She was silent a moment. "David had to have known more than he told us."

"I know." They'd each said it a dozen times since the *Esmeralda*. "Like who our parents were."

Their former protector had been dead for little more than two weeks but it could have been yesterday that he broke them free of the cells beneath the Executioner's Tree. *Of course, now I have to wonder what Williams was up to, sending us there.* It was nearly five years in truth but when Thomas closed his eyes it was no effort at all to slip back into the moment; David's white hair gleaming in torchlight, his different-coloured eyes intent as he hacked through their chains with a hand axe. "Don't look so shocked," he'd chuckled. "Even slaves can get lucky sometimes." His own wrist had borne an hourglass; his tattoo yellow like their own.

Mia sighed. "But why keep it a secret?"

"To protect us? I can't think of any other reason."

"Well, neither can I. And I shouldn't put myself through the same old questions."

"Let's get some sleep," he said. "Maybe you'll dream up the answers."

She laughed softly. "Maybe I will."

Thomas closed his eyes again and breathed deeply, letting the past fall away, sending questions of tomorrow into oblivion at the same time. It could wait, all of it.

***

Dawn came too soon – the knocking of a fist on wood bringing him wide awake. Pale light slipped through the high windows, falling across winking embers in the fireplace. Mia was stirring in her hammock and Thomas stood, attempting to straighten his rumpled clothing as he stumbled to the door. His head was still thick from interrupted sleep, but he managed to get his limbs working at least.

The blonde woman who'd first met them in the village – Sarasi presumably – stood with a tray. On it, two bowls of cold fruit and steaming mugs waited. She smiled when she handed them over, before turning back for the other buildings before Thomas could even thank her.

He took the food inside and placed the tray in his lap. Mia was awake now and the smell of the tea drew her over. He handed her a mug and she took a sip. "I missed this," she said. Next she took a wedge of orange. "I'd almost forgotten what lemon and orange tasted like."

At his own first bite Thomas found himself in agreement when the tart flavour met his tongue. *How long since I've had something like this?* "I thought Williams' stupidity had wiped out the orange."

"Maybe not in the Twilight Islands – if that is where this came from." Mia took another mouthful. "It seems the cavern is still sealed then."

"Let's hope it stays that way." *Elisabeth can stay in there for the rest of her days as far as I'm concerned.*

"What about the *Albion*?" Mia asked. "If we can't convince Captain Hawkins, do you really know how to make a raft?"

He grinned. "We'll find out."

Once they'd eaten, Thomas led Mia to the long stone wharf where they'd been told, with gestures and unfamiliar words, that 'Henri' could be found.

Striding along the walkway, the breeze soothed him as it ruffled his hair. The two villagers who'd helped yesterday stood with Henry, and the three were smiling as they spoke in the language of the village. As Thomas and Mia arrived, Henry sent the brothers upon some errand. Both fellows smiled and nodded to Thomas as they moved off.

"How good are your eyes, Thomas?" Henry asked, still-smiling. Glancing at Mia, his expression fell momentarily, his next words faltering, but Mia waved off his concern when he tried to apologise.

"Henry, don't worry yourself."

"Well, if you're sure," he said, then gestured to the ocean. "Look."

Thomas shaded his eyes and squinted into the distance, was there a tiny shape out there? "The *Albion*?" Could it be? Was their fortune going to hold out a little longer at least? A niggling doubt lingered – a doubt bred of years of disappointment – how long could such luck last them? *Don't question it fool, just enjoy fate's smile for once.*

"That it is," Henry replied. "We have a lookout up the mountain a little way and Walt's spyglass never lies."

Thomas couldn't stop his own smile. "This is wonderful news. Any sign of a breech in the tunnel?"

"None. She'll try her canons but I doubt that will work. We have a man up there, of course, but no signal has come yet."

"And how long until the ship docks?" Mia asked.

"Well within the hour; she's fast."

Henry pointed up to the ridge above the village, the one that contained the mine. "I already have men preparing the jewels and other folk are readying the guest rooms – some of the *Albion*'s crew prefer to stay ashore when they dock, though not all will. Elsewhere, we'll be setting up the square for trading other items. The village is especially keen to get their hands on some more timber."

"You and the captain handle the main exchanges?" Thomas asked.

"We do," he said. "In fact, I'd better prepare myself. You're welcome to wait here if you wish – there'll be quite a crowd soon, so you might want to hold your positions."

Thomas looked to Mia, who was already nodding to him, as if she'd expected his question. She'd folded her arms and was now drumming fingers along her bicep. Yet her energy was not one of apprehension, but of anticipation. *She feels the hope too.*

"We have to convince the captain to take us on," she said.

He nodded. "I don't know anything about sailing but I

can work."

"Maybe they'll need a cook."

"We're going to find out soon," he said. "It's growing larger on the horizon by the minute."

A crowd began to gather while Thomas and Mia waited. They were soon surrounded by smiling faces and excited murmuring, the words indistinct but collectively enough to smother the lap of waves against stone. The sun rose as the *Albion* drew near, a hulking shadow on the glittering water.

When it was close enough to slow and ease toward the long pier, Thomas could only stare. The *Albion* cast a shadow, its iron sides towering above the crowd, twin stacks pumping steam into the sky. Its nose was high and sharp, reinforced as if to ram. Its sides were painted black with blue trim, silver lettering proclaiming her name – *Albion*.

It was magnificent. He explained as best he could to Mia. "The rails are empty but I see gun turrets – it's not unlike the sand-hog, that way. The portholes are dark and closed but I imagine that will change soon."

"How do you board it?" she asked.

A whistle pierced the air as the ship came to dock, figures finally appearing above to lower a ramp to the stones below. A small cheer rose from the crowd but the sailors didn't stop their work. An enormous anchor, shaped as a curved swordfish, plunged into the harbour.

"A long platform," he said. "Probably forty steps."

Villagers helped secure the stair and only then did a tall figure appear at the top. Thomas squinted up at the man. He carried a heavy rifle on one shoulder and wore a cloak. As he descended, Thomas noted that the man had shaved the hair on his head down to skin and when the fellow turned to wave at the sailors behind him, a spiderweb tattooed into the back of his head was revealed.

Thomas tensed.

The man turned back to the crowd, his voice booming. "Very well, you lot. Bring me every last jewel in that mine of yours or I'll wipe you and your village from the face of the very earth."

Chapter 11

Still only halfway down the platform, the man cursed and called for one of the sailors, prodding the man. The fellow spoke falteringly, as if largely unfamiliar with the words, but it was clearly the language used in the village.

His speech caused cries of confusion and fear to swell in the crowd so he'd obviously been understood.

Thomas was already backing away, Mia's hand in his own.

Clearly, something had gone terribly wrong on the ship. *And I'll be damned if that's Captain Hawkins wearing a Bruiser's spiderweb.* Williams' elite enforcement soldiers all wore the tattoo – and maybe 'Bruiser' was a name more befitting a street-thug but there was nothing bumbling or base about those who wore the web.

The Bruiser lifted his rifle and a crack split the air. Laughter followed.

No-one fell; he'd shot into the sky, but the crowd surged away from the ship with a clamour of shouts.

Thomas pulled Mia close, wrapping an arm around her as they were swept along with the press of bodies. Splashes followed as people were knocked from the pier but Thomas kept his feet and only stopped when they were pushed into an opening between the two buildings nearest the harbour.

"He'll know who we are," Mia said.

"I know."

"We can't risk the tunnel."

"We have to hide," Thomas said. More shots sounded from the Albion, the tread of booted feet joining them. The Bruiser's soldiers would have the village subdued within the hour; Thomas hadn't seen anything war-like about the people of Silver Rock.

Henry's voice rose above the din. "Who are you?"

"Does that matter, old man?" the tattooed captain answered. "Bring him with us," he said to someone else. Their voices grew louder and Thomas drew Mia into a crouch behind him. Was it dark enough?

The Bruiser was still speaking. "You're the village elder?"

"I am," Henry replied. "You have no need to make examples of us; we are not warriors here."

"No, you are slaves. And let me give you some advice. If you mean to plan something covert, old man, then remember: those who think themselves heroes will earn no glory, only a grave of saltwater, whereas you might live long as slaves. It should be just like wearing an old shoe for many of you." His snicker was clear as he passed the alley but he did not glance within and neither did Henry.

The old man's face was unresponsive as stone.

Villagers and soldiers were prodded along, the soldiers joking amongst themselves. *Won't be long before they start a proper search.* The stream soon ended and Thomas let a breath escape.

Mia shook his shoulder. "Where do we hide?"

"They'll search all the buildings." He clenched his jaw. There was no-where, they couldn't return to the tunnel and swimming into the ocean was suicide. "The mine?"

"Isn't that why they're here?"

He swore. But there was one place Williams' men wouldn't search – at least not unless they were given a reason.

The *Albion.*

"That's the stupidest idea you've ever had," Mia said when he spoke the thought aloud.

"I know. Do you have anything better?"

Silence. And finally. "No."

"Then we wait until dark and sneak aboard."

"How?"

He clenched and unclenched his hands. How, how, how? *There has to be a way. The ship is probably impenetrable from the outside. But who's going to accept us as soldiers, even if we can steal the proper clothing? It still left climbing the outside.*

He snapped his fingers. "The portholes."

"What?"

"We climb the anchor chain and break in through one of the portholes."

Mia shook her head but said only, "And when we get in there? If it even works?"

"We have to figure that out when we do." He stood slowly, Mia following him. "In the meantime we need a nice empty building with two exits."

"Anything else?" Mia asked.

Booted feet approached. "This way, boys," a voice called.

Thomas drew back into the deeper shadows again but three figures appeared at the mouth of the alley and levelled their rifles – twin-shots, able to punch through the heaviest flak jackets with ease, far more deadly than Thomas' lighter willow rifle – a rifle which lay in his room in any event.

"There you are." The lead soldier spoke softly, yet triumph was clear in his voice.

Thomas raised his hands, keeping his body in front of Mia.

"Aiden will be pleased to find you two of all people, here."

Thomas clenched his jaw. *How do they know who we are just by looking? And in the dark? And how the hell did they know* exactly *where to look?* "We're just travellers."

"And when I check your wrists there'll be no yellow tattoos on you or your sister, right? Save it, Thomas. The King has been looking for you two for far too long. He'll pay a pretty penny indeed, so you're coming with me and if you resist, we'll start on your sister."

A second man added his own threat. "King's bounty says you have to be alive but nothing about what shape you has to be in."

Thomas fought the urge to spit in the man's face. His shoulders trembled but he didn't make a move. There was nothing he could do – he'd failed Mia.

They would be slaves once more.

Chapter 12

Aiden sat in one of Henry's chairs by the fireplace, extending his long legs to rest dusty boots on the low table before Thomas and Mia. The man wore a smirk on his unshaven face and his bald head gleamed in the lantern light. From the current angle, the spiderweb tattoo was just visible, the strands nearing his ears. Up close, silver stubble was visible on his chin though he did not appear truly old.

It had taken all day, held in their room under guard, for the man to decide he was ready to see them. And now it seemed he wasn't going to do anything except stare at them with a self-satisfied expression.

Thomas felt more than saw Mia's frustration beside him, shoulders back, chin lifted. *Perhaps it's better than fear at least.*

"You don't recognise me, do you?" Aiden finally said. He turned to Mia. "The sound of my voice?"

"No," she said.

Thomas glared back at the Bruiser.

Aiden grunted. "Well, David would certainly recall."

"What the hell does that mean?" Mia was on her feet.

Thomas would have reached for her, but after snapping the first set of chains they'd put him in, his hands were now bound to the shackles at his feet; he'd been carried into the room since the binding forced him to hunch forward. The first chains had been old, it seemed, but it still gave the soldiers enough concern to take extra precautions with him. Mia was bound too, but only with rope at her wrists.

The Bruiser grinned up at her. "Careful now, if you keep that up you might learn things about him that you wouldn't like."

"David was a good man," Thomas said quietly.

"Thank you for clearing that up," Aiden said. "Now, whether you remember me or not is immaterial, since you'll be heading back to the capital tomorrow in any event. His majesty is most interested in you both."

"Why?" Thomas asked. Maybe Aiden wanted to gloat – if so, let the fool, so long as it offered some useful information. The claims of knowing them, of knowing David could be set aside for the moment, troubling as they were.

"Because you are unique among many. And more importantly, because he thinks he can use you."

"You doubt him?"

"Not really; he uses everyone," Aiden said. "That's how he survives. And it doesn't matter to me. All that matters to me is that I get my gold."

"Unique how?" Mia asked.

"You're better suited to answer than I am, aren't you?"

Thomas frowned. Damn this Aiden and his cryptic questions. *Just what is this bastard hiding?*

"He doesn't know anything," Mia said, disappointment – and derision – clear in her voice.

Aiden straightened. "Don't goad me, woman. I know plenty. And just because you two were the Alchemist's pets doesn't make you better than me. Don't forget who wears the Hourglass."

Thomas leaned closer. Pets? "Who is the Alchemist?"

"You of all people should know the legendary Silas." Aiden snapped his fingers at the doorway, and two soldiers entered, one the man who found them in the alley. "Introduce them to Captain Hawkins."

"Yes, sir."

Thomas was hauled to his feet and half-carried, half-shoved toward the exit, hobbling as best he could. Aiden's voice followed him.

"Maybe it's best that you don't remember me, after all." It seemed a trace of regret lingered in his words.

Thomas couldn't turn to respond and Mia didn't seem inclined to answer either, besides which, they were already being herded down the hall and toward the front door. *What does he know about us? And why can't I remember someone called Silas?*

***

He'd been prodded up the walkway and across the hardwood decks, past the rail and the polished steel of the Gatlings, into the nearest door. The entry sat beneath the shadow of the mighty stacks where they loomed above.

A steep ladder waited within the doorway and he navigated it with great difficulty only, crashing to the floor after mistiming the final few steps. He swore, rubbing at his knees as best he could.

"Thomas?" Mia asked.

"I'm fine," he replied.

"Shut up," one of the soldiers snapped. He lifted Thomas again and pushed him toward another door at the end of a dim passage. This revealed a second ladder. Thomas groaned and the other soldier muttered about wasting time.

"Then separate my arms from the leg shackles," Thomas growled.

"Not likely."

Another tedious climb and another long corridor, this one lined with portholes. He caught only glimpses of the moon-lit coast, but it was enough to see a furnace of lights above the town where the mouth to the mine lay. It seemed Aiden was rushing to collect as many gemstones as he could before leaving. No doubt working Henry and the rest of Silver Rock to the bone to do it. *And we're powerless to help. Worse, maybe our coming here doomed them to it.*

Finally, the first man pulled them to a halt before a heavy steel door and produced a key. Once he had the door open, he shoved Thomas inside. He crashed to the steel floor with a grunt, Mia thumping into him a moment later.

The men cackled with laughter as the door swung shut, leaving Thomas and Mia in darkness, save for three circles of light that streaked down from high portholes like thin bullets of moonlight.

"Sorry," Mia said as she pushed herself off him.

"Don't be."

"Maybe I should have tried to call the bird. Before they took us."

"No. The light would have brought more men down on us." He rolled himself upright and gripped the chains, pulling at them where those binding his hands were connected to the links spanning his feet. He grunted with the effort. Nothing.

"What are you doing?"

"I'm going to break these and then we're going to find Captain Hawkins and his men and we're taking his ship back. Then, once we drive Aiden and *his* men into the ocean, we'll sail to Europa and live the rest of our lives in peace," he said. "Sounds simple, doesn't it?"

"Yes."

"Hope you've got a plan to go with all that bravado, lad." The voice was weary, speaking from across the room, its owner lost in shadow.

Mia startled. "Who are you?" she asked, concern in her tone.

"Hawkins. And I have no men, not anymore. The scum Bruiser had them cast overboard." Now bitterness was clear. His voice was deep, seeming to fill the space.

"We can work together," Thomas said. "What do you say, Captain?"

"Free yourself first and we'll talk, lad."

Thomas dragged himself toward a circle of light where it fell onto the wall, illuminating a hook. With some difficulty, he looped his ankle chains over the hook then leant back, letting it take the strain. Next, he gripped the chains that bound his wrists and pulled, using the leverage of the hook.

Steel scraped against steel. He kept the pressure on, muscles in his arms and shoulders stiffening as he fought the chains. They dug into his skin, grinding against tendon and bone and he grimaced. *This is probably a waste of bloody time. These chains aren't old like the other set.*

Yet he didn't stop. Would not stop.

Heat built in his muscles... something unlike the usual

effects of exertion and a strange sense of familiarity came over him with it. As if he was *meant* to break the steel. But it was not a premonition or a sensation of the future like Mia sometimes had, it was something else. He strained harder.

"Come on," he gasped.

The chain held.

Thomas threw his head back, straining with his whole body now – the shackle on one ankle tight against the hook. The heat intensified, building as it spread along his limbs, as if fire surged beneath his skin. But no new light filled the room, only his laboured breathing.

"Thomas, you'll hurt yourself," Mia said.

He couldn't answer; it was almost as if the heat lent him strength. If he stopped he'd never break free and it seemed the chain was starting to—

A loud snap filled the room. His head flew back, thumping into the floor.

Thomas groaned as his vision swam.

Someone was speaking yet the haze swallowed the words. Pain slowly seeped into his awareness, spreading from the back of his head. It crept further, streaking around to his eyes. The light from the porthole blazed. He screwed his eyes shut but the pain did not fade.

It burrowed deeper and he raised both hands to grip his temples, curling into a ball where he lay. *What the hell is happening?* Something was trying to split his skull from the inside.

And then nothing.

He rolled onto his back, chest heaving.

"Thomas, answer me!" Someone shook his shoulder.

"I hear you."

"What happened?" Mia asked.

"I don't know," he said between gasps. "There was heat and pain... in my head. Pain. It was..." He swallowed, unable to finish.

She put her head upon his chest, hugging him as best she could with her own bindings. "You did it, you know. I can't believe it but you broke the chains."

"What?"

She sat up. "See for yourself."

Thomas lifted his head, moving slowly. Was his entire body about to fall to pieces? He tried moving his torso and his head didn't explode. Chains clinked, loud in the hush. From his sitting position he could see his ankles were no longer bound together. Pieces of the chain still hung from the manacles but he'd be able to walk freely. He reached for the shattered link, the edges rough beneath his thumb – and it hit him. *My hands are free too.*

He still sported the manacles and twin tails of chain links but he was essentially free.

How?

Thomas stared at the link he held. It looked so normal, even broken – the piece was hard, unyielding. Cold. Just like steel ought to have been. Yet his flesh had somehow shattered the link – he was stronger than steel. And the heat... where did it come from? *What's happening to me?*

"Thomas?" a note of worry had entered her voice.

There wasn't time to dwell on what had happened; there was still a job to do.

"Give me your hands," he said.

Mia held them out, wrists bound. Thomas took the sharpened chain link and began to saw through her ropes.

Once she was free, he stood and moved across the room, taking careful steps, heading for the dark shape of the captain.

Thomas knelt beside the man. "Ready to fight back?"

Captain Hawkins leant into the moonlight, the whites of his eyes brighter against the darkness. "You broke those chains with your hands?" He wore a sweeping moustache and dried blood was black in his fair hair; bruises extended down one side of his face. He was a tall man, his legs pulled almost up to his chest in the cramped confines of where he'd been chained to the wall – chains binding his torso. Thomas doubted the man had been able to move much beyond what he managed now, at any time during his confinement. Boxes, supplies of some manner, hemmed the man in.

"I suppose I did. Let's see how I do with yours."

Mia's hand found his back; she adjusted her grip and pulled upon his shoulder. "Should you wait a little? Recover your strength?"

"Maybe... but we might not have much time."

Hawkins grinned now. "If you can free me we've struck a deal – I'll let you help me take back this ship."

"And then you'll take us anywhere we ask," Mia said with a sniff.

He chuckled. "Consider it done."

"You're giving us your word?" Thomas asked.

"Aye. If you help get me my ship back I'll be in your debt, I swear it now." There was a conviction in the words that Thomas didn't believe the man could fake. And Mia hadn't objected either; it was probably safe to trust him.

"All right." Thomas gripped the chains in both hands but hesitated. If he simply dragged at one end, he'd tighten them and crush Hawkins' ribcage. In order to snap the chains, Thomas had to pull them apart by spreading his arms. *No small feat, that.*

He flexed his fingers and gripped the links tight, pulling them. They held. He applied more pressure, bracing himself as best he could in the narrow confines, muscles protesting. Yet the heat returned more swiftly this time and his strength didn't flag. Instead, the chains seemed weaker than his own, trembling beneath his assault.

"That's it," Hawkins said. "Keep going."

Thomas clenched his teeth and redoubled his efforts. His vision began to dim but he refused to stop. *No. I can do this too.*

The chain burst.

Steel ricocheted from the wall. Sparks flashed and a piece lodged into the crate behind him as he toppled to his knees, breathing hard once again. He held himself up with one hand, the other roamed his chest, seeking wounds. But no piece of chain had found him and Mia had already put her arms around him again, her voice full of concern. "Thomas?"

"I'm fine," he said.

The sound of rattling chains followed. Thomas glanced up to find Hawkins holding out his hand. "Let's take my ship back."

Chapter 13

The heavy steel door had defeated them.

Not Thomas' new-found strength, not Mia's failed attempts to bring the bird of light into the hold, nor Hawkins' knowledge of his own ship had been able to free them. The night wore on and every effort to breach the door, failed. Thomas' jaw ached from being clenched – he'd broken the chains before, why couldn't he break through the door now? Neither the strange tingling nor the warmth he'd felt before returned. Had he exhausted whatever mysterious new strength he'd unlocked?

Nothing in the room could help either. The supplies were no more than foodstuffs and cloth once bound for Silver Rock. Climbing up them to a porthole was of no use; it was too small for even Mia to squeeze through.

When dawn light brushed the glass and the deep rumble of the boiler began, Hawkins slumped against the wall. "And so we return to Birnhale and that bastard Williams finally gets his filthy hands on my ship."

Thomas leant against the wall, still enjoying being able to

stretch out, while Mia sat beside him on one of the barrels. "He's been searching for a long time?"

"Years. And when your friend Aiden tries to collect the bounty you mentioned, Williams will have what he wants."

"Wait," Mia said. "Williams didn't send Aiden here? Didn't send him after you?"

The captain shook his head. "No. That Bruiser has his own crew and they're in this for themselves. They think they're pirates, that they'll plunder every port but they're stone fools if they think they can sneak in and out of the capital."

"What went wrong with Aiden?" Mia asked, her voice hushed.

Hawkins was quiet a moment, his gaze trained on his boots before he tossed a chain link he'd been toying with to one side. It clattered into the shadows. "I still don't know. I've been turning it over in my mind for days now and I cannot figure it. He knew things that only a crew member should have known." He shrugged. "They ambushed us in the wilds of Old Asia – we only make the trip once a year. Would have taken that bastard half a year to even *plan* the job."

"You think one of your men betrayed you?"

"I don't want to think it. They were handpicked, all of them. But if one was a traitor, he got what he deserved first day out from the ruined docks." He folded his arms. "The rest of my men, however, Aiden owes a great debt."

"We'll find a way," Thomas said.

"Then we'd better do it quickly."

"How long do we have?" Mia asked.

"Permit me some pride here," Captain Hawkins said,

sitting just a little straighter. "But the Albion could reach the capital in three days if the boilers run nonstop."

Thomas gave a low whistle. That sort of speed... nothing could compare. As best he could estimate they were two thousand kilometres from the capital and it had taken them many weeks to travel so far. Admittedly, there had been diversions and a whole day and night hidden in a cave but still... "Then we have three days to find a way to stop Aiden."

Yet by midday they'd come up with no plan deemed worthy. "Being trapped in here is what it comes down to," Hawkins said. "We need to open that door and there's no way it's going to happen."

As if to reinforce his point, a hatch in the door snapped open and a tray was slid inside, scraping across the floor. On it, three flasks of water, hard bread and several pieces of orange. Whoever had delivered it did not speak.

Thomas divided the food and water; both were welcome but his mood was only elevated slightly, despite the pleasant tangy flavour to the fruit. There had to be a way. *If Aiden cares about the bounty he'll save us if he thinks we're in danger – but the sick prisoner trick? He'd see through it.*

No better ideas came by nightfall. He forced down the ache in his stomach and eventually, at Hawkins' and Mia's insistence, stopped his pacing, lying down to rest on a bed of fabrics arranged from the supplies. Yet sleep was slow to come; he turned often, his mind racing with plans and curses on Aiden, on Williams, on them all. Mia seemed to fare no better; he could hear her sigh often from where she lay nearby. It was a soft sound, as if she sought to hide her fear and frustration from him.

The next day was just the same, the distant hum of the

boiler, a single meal and no progress on escape. By noon of the third day, no-one spoke unless it was to offer a suggestion. Yet each was denied as implausible. Hawkins had already smashed a crate to pieces in an outburst of frustration – Thomas could have joined him.

Finally the *Albion* slowed and came to a halt, rumble of the engines growing quiet. Had they docked already? The boiler still hummed and Thomas thought the swell of the city had now joined it, the rhythmic thump and clanging of factories that lined the harbour. Was the sky through the porthole scuffed with steam and smoke and the rest of the bile that Birnhale pumped into the air?

The thought turned his stomach but he climbed up to peer through nonetheless.

Birnhale lay curled around a murky bay, climbing up into the hills above. Smoke and steam from stone factories hung over the city like an endless reminder of the work produced here – even on the stone docks he could see small steam-cars with their heavy wheels rattling along. Other machines toiled on the wharves, mechanical arms lifting goods from smaller ships, puffing steam as they did. Yet the smog was so thick, the air too still to banish it. The domed, walled Fortress and arena were no more than dark shapes looming above the homes and shops.

The streets were set in squares and some climbed the hills and concealed small gardens, old places that had been dying for as long as he'd been alive. And the closer you were to the bay the narrower, darker, and more spiteful the streets became. It wasn't just the bitterness or despair of those cursed with the white or black hourglass; the factory-slaves who rarely seemed to see the sun, it was the thieves, charlatans and free merchants who dealt in items even Williams wanted stopped. Like the drugs. *Years since I've even seen a powder-rat.*

"Well?" Mia asked.

"It's Birnhale," he said heavily. "And it's as grimy as ever."

She muttered beneath her breath. "Can you see the Fortress?"

"Too much smog." Not that he wanted to see it; they'd already spent too much time there. *And I won't go back either. They'll have to drag me.* Yet denying a new curiosity was difficult – would Silas and answers wait within? Or had Williams done away with the man in a famous fit of rage?

"What do we do now, then?" Mia asked.

"Wait for Aiden to come, then strike. Quickly," he added. "Can you call the bird?"

She nodded. "I think so. And then?"

He shook his head. "I don't know." Thomas arranged himself near the door, just to its left and guided Mia to another hiding place with some directions, but she didn't seem to need his voice. Hawkins waved off any concern.

"Let them see me first, supposedly bound. If any come close enough, I'll have a surprise for them."

"Just don't look at the light," Thomas said.

"What light?"

"If it happens, you'll know. Mia will sing. I can't really explain it."

Hawkins shrugged. "Then show me when the time comes. I'll be ready."

Thomas crossed the floor to Mia a moment. "Will Hawkins and I be blinded, so close to the bird?"

"Just look away, like before."

"All right." Thomas returned to his position near the door. And then they waited.

He tapped his boot and waited some more.

Finally, footsteps approached. The sound of several men. He held his breath as Mia started to sing the lullaby. A key rattled in the lock. Mia's voice grew louder. Someone cursed from beyond the steel, as if struggling with the lock. Yet no bird appeared. A note of concern entered Mia's voice. *It's not going to work. Damn it.* Thomas tensed as the door swung open. A soldier stepped into the room; he'd barely managed half a step when Thomas yanked the man from his feet, hurling him into a wall. The gun clattered from his grip where the fellow lay groaning, and Thomas dived for it. His hand clasped the shaft when a voice rang out.

"Halt."

Aiden stood in the doorway, a revolver in hand. The man's frown was quite deep and he waved two men into the room to help the first soldier to his feet, and to collect the weapon. One of the men kicked Thomas in the ribs and Thomas grunted.

Mia, her expression one of fear, rushed forth.

"I'm fine," he said as he rose and folded his arms. "Stay back, Mia."

The Bruiser gestured with his chin. "However you got yourself free has proved to be a waste of time. You're going to be deposited at William's doormat and I will have my money."

"Want us to re-chain him?" one of the other soldiers asked.

"I have a better idea."

Aiden swung the gun to Mia and pulled the trigger.

The shot boomed in the confines of the hold and Mia

cried out, collapsing to grip her thigh. Blood bloomed between her fingers. Her lip bled too – she'd cut it with her teeth.

Thomas charged.

Rage consumed him, blood thundering in his ears but he'd only taken two steps when Aiden swung the barrel back to Thomas. "Think! If you die, your sister dies."

Thomas clenched his jaw, arms trembling. The man was insane. A shot to the thigh was a huge risk; Mia could bleed out before they even reached Williams.

"Williams has the best doctors in the whole nation – you know that, you've doubtless seen them," Aiden continued. "Cooperate and she'll get there in time. Fail to do so and she won't. Choose quickly."

Thomas trembled. *The bastard's right.* "Fine. You win," Thomas ground out.

Aiden smiled, almost lazily, as if he'd known exactly what Thomas would do.

Chapter 14

Somewhere, voices argued about still needing Captain Hawkins but Thomas couldn't tear his focus away from Mia where she lay across the back seat of one of the royal steam-cars. Sweat beaded at her brow, dampening her hair. She was pale, her breathing shallow.

He'd made a bandage as best he could and the bleeding seemed to slow but every bump in the road caused her to groan as she fell in and out of consciousness. Whenever her grip on his hand slackened his heart squeezed itself into a sickening ball in his chest.

Outside the steam-car, the city slums that crouched beyond the cacophonous factories rolled by – shadows long and walls covered in grime, doors boarded up and beggars clinging to the lamp poles or corners, their dirty faces thin and pale. *This is taking too long.*

"Go faster," he demanded.

"Shut your mouth." Aiden glanced back from where he sat beside the driver, a man who Thomas could not describe beyond the glimpses of brown leather gloves on the steering wheel. "We go as fast as these pitiful streets allow."

"She's in pain," Thomas said, leaning to point at the man. "If she dies, I'll—"

"Do nothing," Aiden replied. "You're a slave; slaves don't get to do anything. You better remember that when we reach the Fortress."

"If Mia dies Williams will kill you – and if he doesn't, I will."

"Are you sure of that?"

Mia groaned again and Thomas tore his glare from Aiden and stroked her forehead. Her mouth flashed open and she gasped but said nothing. Thomas patted her hand and glanced back out the window – the slums were gone now, the steam-car picking up speed. Taller buildings filled his vision, clean glass and beautiful items within but he could not recall the colour or shape of a single one after it passed.

He turned back to Mia and lowered his voice. "Hold on."

When the Fortress finally appeared ahead he was straining to keep from slamming his fist into the back of the driver's seat. Mia was still breathing but she no longer groaned when the wheels hit uneven road.

When the steam-car drew to a stop, Aiden opened his door and waved for soldiers to flank him, Thomas saw it all on his periphery. His attention was fixed on Mia. *You can't die, sis. I need you.*

"Bring her."

Thomas looked up, Aiden was waiting. The spiderweb glanced at Mia and a flicker of doubt crossed his features, but it was replaced by a stony impatience so quickly that Thomas wasn't sure whether he'd imagined it or not.

Thomas stepped out then lifted Mia into his arms.

They stood in the broad entryway, flagstones and stone columns ahead as the Fortress towered over him. This close, all he could see were clawed gargoyles on the roof spouts above and the long corridor before him.

"We'll be escorted directly to Williams or one of his snivelling sons. Act like a slave and maybe you'll both survive. Walk."

"Williams wants us for something – we'll both survive," Thomas said as he started after Aiden. "Will you?" So far, Mia seemed to be holding on.

The ex-Bruiser grunted. He was surrounded by a dozen of his own heavily-armed men, their faces grim. They were, in turn, being escorted by at least twice as many soldiers – these also bearing serious weaponry but wearing the grey and silver of the King's personal guardsmen.

"And now he'll have you and then Hawkins' ship too."

Aiden laughed. "Williams won't lay a finger on my ship – I've got all the leverage I need on him."

"What does that mean?"

"I know you're not asking me that because you believe I'd actually tell you."

Thomas kept pace but asked no more questions.

Mia's chest rose and fell – shallow but regular enough. The sweat was worsening and she still did not respond when he said her name. Their progress slowed as the halls narrowed – not significantly, but enough that such a large group of men could no longer move swiftly. The walls were lined with paintings, alternating with tall windows. Each image sat within a heavy golden frame, depicting one Williams ancestor or another. They all bore the similar features, deep-set eyes and cruel mouths. There was a strength there too, an iron will.

Thomas couldn't hold back a snort of derision. *You're all scum, every last one of you.*

Aiden glanced over his shoulder but did not speak, though his expression seemed to suggest a certain amount of agreement.

"He's no King," Thomas said. "His whole line, all the supposed lords and ladies, they're all false – there's not a noble bone in a single body around here. And nothing even close to nobility has set foot in here for centuries."

"That sounds like David talking."

Maybe it was. "I don't think you disagree, Bruiser."

"You're right; I don't think he's a King."

"Yet you accept him as one."

Aiden shook his head. "I admit he operates just like one, and that's close enough when you get right down to it, isn't it?"

"No."

"Well, if his family hadn't got their grubby little mitts on the slave trade all those years ago you'd be cursing someone else's name now but you'd still be a slave, so there's little difference in the end."

Thomas swallowed back a retort.

One of the King's men didn't seem inclined to do so, however. He raised his voice to be heard from beyond the ring Aiden's men. "He is more noble than you, traitor."

Aiden only laughed at the man.

Thomas glanced into the courtyard, where a pair of men in fine dark suits with white gloves sat and gossiped over tea. They were surrounded by greenery peppered with sweet flowers, the scent drifting even into the corridor. *Bastards.*

The windows on the other side of the long passage revealed a similar scene on a grander scale, a long table of clean white cloth. For now, it was empty of guests but young boys and girls ran around setting plates and cutlery, one perched on a chair to adjust flowers in a vase at the centre. Each child bore the yellow hourglass and wore the same harried expression – something Thomas remembered well. *You deserve better.*

At last they reached a bare antechamber where their footfalls clapped on marble floors. Huge double doors were closed but a secondary passage stood open. One of Williams' men pointed. "This way. Your men will have to stay here."

Aiden nodded to his second – the man who'd found Thomas and Mia in the alley – and they remained behind as the Bruiser strode ahead. Thomas followed the man and two of Williams' guards down a long, twisting, dimly-lit corridor and into a room lined with wooden panels. It could have been oak, or something equally rare.

A man sat before a workbench, a series of cogs, springs and tiny instruments spread before him, gleaming beneath the light of a desk-lamp. A large magnifying glass hung before the man. Its mechanical arm creaked when he pushed it back and regarded them with dark, deep-set eyes.

King Williams.

He had aged. Grey stubble covered his face and deep lines ran from mouth to chin. His knuckles appeared swollen when he stood, brushing metal shavings from his rumpled coat and vest, the crimson silk creased, ruined.

"Now here are three faces I have long hoped to see once more." His voice filled the room, gravelly where it was once sharp and cutting, where it had once chilled Thomas. As a child, desperate to perform to the exacting standards of the Fortress, he'd once trembled at the very mention of Williams' name. Flinched whenever the King passed by – and in all that time, it seemed the man barely noticed him. Or Mia.

Yet the King regarded them now.

But this time, Thomas was no child. "Find her a doctor."

Williams blinked, then chuckled. "Let us do just that." He gestured to one of his lackeys. "Make haste; she must survive."

The man turned and ran from the room.

Thomas started after him but William's voice cracked out with all the power it had seemed to lack before. "Slave!"

Thomas froze, cursing himself for falling back into old habits.

"You will wait – Anderson will take her."

Their guide reached out and Thomas handed Mia over after a moment's hesitation. *She'll survive. She must. Williams needs her foresight, his doctors are the best.* The words became a silent chant as he watched Anderson hurry after the first man.

"Aiden, I am disappointed."

"I bet you are, old man."

The King frowned. "This is a poor attempt at an apology. After all, you are here to beg for my forgiveness."

Now Aiden sneered. "I am here for the bounty on the big guy and his sister. You can send it to the *Albion* before I depart, which is within the hour," he said, and started to leave.

Williams crossed the room, his grip snapping over Aiden's shoulder. "You are a fool."

"No, *your majesty*. You are the fool." Rage filled Aiden's

voice. "Not all have forgotten the debts you owe in the west."

The King's hand fell away. "You cannot lay claim to such a debt."

"I can and I do," Aiden replied. "Ask her yourself if you doubt me."

He strode toward the exit, pausing to glance at Thomas before leaving. "Your sister will be fine." Williams simply stood and stared after the man, a look Thomas had never thought to see on the King's face.

Fear.

A deep fear that suddenly aged the man more than mere wrinkles and grey hair could achieve.

Chapter 15

Thomas was unable to convince the guards to skip his own medical treatment – which he hardly needed for scrapes and bruises – and when he finally sat beside Mia's bed, he found himself blinking back sleep despite his worry. Even the irritatingly bright lamp wasn't enough to banish his drowsiness. It was like a persistent demon, dragging downward on his limbs, his head and his eyelids. But he couldn't let it win, he had to be awake in case she stirred and needed him.

She breathed evenly now, tucked beneath white sheets. Her hair was midnight-black against the white pillow. He'd almost forgotten how clean the place was. But the bright, soft fabric was just another luxury in the Fortress with a hidden human cost. *Not that a single Lord or Lady would even care that it took us hours working over chemical baths that seared our lungs to prepare these fabrics.*

The doctor returned, carrying a vial. He wore a white coat with a giant red serpent coiled around a cross – an ancient symbol of his profession. The man was short; large spectacles lay across his nose, and the fellow would have appeared quite comical if Thomas let the humour come to the fore but his mind refused the inclination.

"When she wakes, have her drink this," the doctor said, handing the vial over. Thomas straightened to accept it. Pale green liquid sloshed within the glass. "It will ease her pain and help her heal."

"Thank you, Doctor."

He nodded before moving to leave, then turned back. "Silas was insistent that I accept his help but I believe it will offer an impressive recovery and I am quite interested in the results."

Thomas stood. "The alchemist?"

"Yes. Don't be concerned. He's quite remarkable," the doctor said as he left the room, closing the door behind him. The sound of a bolt sliding home followed. Two guards were posted beyond the door but Thomas hadn't been able to focus on them, on thoughts of escape, until he was certain Mia was well.

But news of the alchemist taking an interest in them once more... was it cause for concern? What role had Silas played in their past? *And if it was as large as Aiden insinuated, why can't we remember it? God damn it, why can't I learn any more than hints and whispers!*

"Thomas?"

Mia turned her head, eyes as sightless as ever, and her hand slipped from beneath the covers, reaching out.

He took it, holding it tight, and smiled, relief washing over him. "I'm here."

"Where are we? I remember... Aiden." She winced. "My leg."

"I know. I have medicine here."

She ran her other hand over the sheets. Her voice dropped. "Thomas... only one place has blankets this fine."

"I'm working on a way out." But he had no ideas, not yet.

"Has he seen us?"

Thomas didn't need to ask who she meant. "Yes. He still wants us, though I still don't know exactly why. His doctor has tended to you. He's expecting a recovery and we've been given medicine that he and the alchemist cooked up. I think it's probably safe."

Mia wiped her forehead. "You don't sound too convinced."

"Well, I should be... why would they heal you most of the way only to harm you now?"

"Just because we cannot see a reason doesn't mean it isn't there."

"True enough."

Mia shifted her head, as if something was bothering her. She reached beneath the pillow and her mouth opened.

"What's wrong – is it your thigh?"

"No, there's something here." She drew forth a crimson key on a slender silver chain, which she ran her fingertips over. "Wait, I thought I dreamt this – it was Aiden, he had to have put this here."

"Aiden? Why – and when?" *While I was being tended to, probably.* Did it explain why the Bruiser had paused to offer a few words of reassurance before leaving? Just *how* did Aiden know them?

"I seemed to remember raised voices, arguing over me. When they stopped I think I was in this room, he spoke my name and mentioned this. He said it would..." she trailed off, a furrow in her brow. "Something about... tomorrow, unlocking tomorrow. There was more but I can't remember it all. It doesn't make sense, I know."

"It makes about as much sense as a rat in a suit but we'll figure it out. Keep it hidden." He told her of the exchange between Aiden and Williams. "Maybe it's something we can use."

She reached up to lock the chain at the back of her neck, the key hidden beneath her shirt. "So what was that plan of yours?"

"Steal a steam-car and flee south to Viterra. That airship is supposed to be there in the wastes and I doubt we'll ever see Hawkins or the *Albion* again."

"Even if the airship is there, we need to get out of the palace and the Fortress first. And after that, the city."

"That's where my plan needs a bit of work," he admitted with a yawn.

Mia tilted her head. "You're tired, why don't you rest. How late is it?"

"Late." He stood, placing the medicine onto a bedside table, before the lamp. "I've left Silas' medicine here if your pain worsens." Yet he did not move to the second bed, even though it looked soft. The temptation was great... but if he wasn't awake to watch over her, who knew what might happen? Williams was hardly predictable.

"Thomas, rest. I'll call if I need you. We're already enslaved again. What else can go wrong?"

"Don't tempt fate, sister." But he moved to the bed where he slumped down and kicked off his boots.

"Just do as I say without grumbling, for once."

"All right." Thomas lay back and let his head sink into the pillow, the soft feathers within almost too pliable. His body sank into the mattress, just enough to give the illusion of a cloud – or so he liked to imagine.

Sleep came swiftly, despite the sliver of worry that something could happen the moment he closed his eyes.

***

Thomas folded his arms, fighting a sneer.

Williams stood upon the Fortress walls, the great dome of steel and rust rising up behind him, his expression one of pride as he pointed across the city. "The factory to the left of the old cathedral is new. It produces twin-shot canons and the ammunition. By the end of the summer, we will have enough to finally put down the Inland Federation once and for all."

"They are no threat to us," Thomas snapped. Nor had they been for years; their border was closed and while they remained a haven for runaway slaves, the Federation was not rich in resources. Last Thomas heard, they were fighting a famine. Mia stood nearby, leaning against the dome, leg wrapped in bandages. She was listening but an expression of discomfort rested on her face – from her wound or the King? *Probably both.*

"How short-sighted of you," Williams said. "Understand, from force comes safety. We will crush them."

A steady wind blew cool air up from the bay, clearing the haze of smoke and letting the sun burst through to wash the buildings with its light, setting the steel and polished brass to gleaming, obscuring the murkier aspects of Birnhale. The same wind stirred the King's hair and the crimson and grey clothing he wore. This time, the garments were clean and free of crease lines.

"You must be so thrilled," Mia said.

He turned to face her. "Indeed. We will soon enter an era of stability such has not been seen for decades," he said, either not recognising her sarcasm or ignoring it completely.

"Under your boot heel," she said.

"Not all are born to rule – such freedom is tantamount to chaos."

"Nor were you," Thomas said.

Williams lowered his voice to a familiar growl. "Do not make the mistake of thinking you are as useful to me as your sister, Thomas."

Thomas flinched.

The king continued. "Further east I'm sure you can see the arena – it is closed now. I am using it to build my greatest single creation, something that will further cement my family's rule for generations to come – and more, protect us from the foreign devils who seek to take what is ours."

"Who?" Mia asked.

"Those from Europa or Chinese-Russia, it does not matter. They all seek what we have."

Thomas didn't answer, though he could have laughed at the claim. The other nations of the world had turned their backs on Williams' Brasatalis; they did not seek any part of it.

"Why tell us your vision for the future?" Mia asked. "You sent Elisabeth after us, besides your family, she's your second in command. We are two slaves, gone for years. Why do we deserve such special treatment? Why are we of use?"

"Do not worry, you will see Elisabeth again soon enough. I'm sure you both remember her well from your time here before. But it is your gifts, Mia's especially, that are of great interest to me and my line."

Thomas met the man's sunken eyes, the impact of the words taking a moment to register. When they did, he took a step forward. "No."

Mia's expression was enough for him to see she, too, understood.

Williams did not fly into a rage as expected, though Thomas was certain that years ago, he would have. Instead, his voice remained calm. "I will provide for the future and your sister will be a part of that. With my son's mechanical gifts, gifts which outweigh even mine, and Mia's foresight, they will create a dynasty that unites the entire world."

Mia folded her arms. "I will not submit to this."

"When you see the good it will bring, you will change your mind," Williams said.

"I disagree," Mia replied before Thomas could say the same.

If the king was speaking of his eldest son, Julian, Thomas would kill the man first. *Hell, doesn't matter which son – I'd kill Warrick too.* But he couldn't deny an old hatred lingered for Julian, his one-time tormentor. Julian had been the one above the others; the bastard who'd used anything and anyone around him to make life in the palace a misery.

Including Leah.

No. Don't think about that now.

"You will be taken to the arena. There you will see." The King's smile was assured. "It represents the very pinnacle of mankind's scientific knowledge. It is the legacy you and my son must protect. And so, too, must it be your fate, Thomas. Your strength will be harnessed in this task."

"My strength?"

"Surely you have discovered that you are stronger than most?"

Thomas offered no reply.

Williams laughed, a rasping sound. "No need to play coy. I was there when Silas mixed his concoctions."

"What does that mean?"

"You'll have a chance to speak to Silas when I say, no sooner," Williams said. "And now you are going to the arena. You have much to learn."

"Mia's leg is not ready for such a long walk," Thomas said.

"You forget, young Thomas. I am king here – the finest of everything is at my beck and call. No-one will have to walk, especially not our precious Mia."

Chapter 16

The steam-car was much more opulent than the last; it had fine leather upholstery, treated in red with a grey trim lining the windows. Outside, a series of heavy springs provided a far smoother ride; it was, as the king had promised, the finest. Even the boiler was smaller than Thomas had expected, fed water by an automated unit.

The carriage was also more spacious. Petr, the King's lackey who'd been chosen as escort, was able to sit quite comfortably across from them, another soldier at his side. Two men drove, while two more clung to the back of the steam-car. All were armed with revolvers and rifles and all had orders to keep a close eye on Williams' two most important slaves.

Now that the busy streets were sliding by and there was finally some distance between him and the king, Thomas had begun to consider escape. Vague ideas of slipping into the tunnels beneath the arena, if a chance presented itself, came to mind. The problem would be creating the chance. Mia, too, was no doubt thinking on escape, though he could hardly discuss anything with her. At least she didn't seem to be in too much pain. *Silas' concoction is working then.*

They passed other cars and even the occasional horse – rare in the city – along with lines and lines of people heading for markets, or hauling boxes and barrels. Most were factory workers in drab, worn clothing, with hats pulled low over their eyes. There was an oddness to the way they walked; slightly hunched as if trying to escape notice, yet there was a belligerence to their bearing too. As if seeking an excuse to explode – bitterness of a life enslaved was still stronger than despair. Thomas had seen his share of that too.

More guards checked on their car at the arena, but Petr had only to mention the King's business to have everyone waved through the check point and up the broad path toward the arena itself.

Brass statues lined the walkway, Williams in his prime: his eyes just as sunken but his shoulders a little broader. His hands were empty where they'd once held flags, each bearing the symbol or name of teams of combatants favoured by the lords and ladies who watched. 'Common' folk also watched but the only slaves allowed within were those foolish enough to gamble their lives for a slim chance at freedom – testing new, dangerous weapons that harmed the user as often as not. It wasn't Thomas' idea of the best chance at liberty.

But now the statues were empty, cast dark in the great shadow of the arena.

The stone walls climbed a dozen storeys high, rivalling the Fortress. The spiralling windows, those that had once glowed with lamplight of an evening, were paved up, newer brick at odds with the wind-worn grey stone.

"Wonder if Charlie will be on the gate," one of the guards

asked Petr.

"Why? You think he's going to send his sister your way in exchange for more of that poison from your powder-rat friends?"

The first man grunted in protest. "It's worth a shot."

"No, it isn't. Anyone but me and you'd be executed by now – give that rot-gut away, Robert. It'll kill you before you're thirty, and if the King's spies find you with it..."

Robert laughed. "I know, I know. I'll disappear into the bowels of the Fortress and come back as something else. I never believed those stories, you know."

"Well I do," Petr said. "So lay off Charlie. I don't want anyone to overhear you."

Robert grumbled but seemed to agree.

Just how many soldiers used the powder? It hadn't been that way in the past. Thomas looked to Mia, who'd turned to him – in the bright morning sun she would have been able to pick his outline at least, but it wasn't the same as if she had her vision restored all the way. Her blindfold was new; a slightly heavier fabric to deal with the bright sun – a dark yellow silk from the King. She had wanted to cast it aside but Thomas caught her wrist. "Use it. It'll be softer against your skin."

"I don't want anything from him."

"And I don't want you to suffer needlessly, even in a small way," he'd said, perhaps a little too strongly, but she'd relented.

The gates, half again as tall as a house, stood closed. They were burnished steel but that did not make them ornamental, it took a dozen men on each wing to move the gates if the boiler was cold. An hourglass, the sands even between chambers, spanned the two sides of the gate.

Beneath, engraved in bold letters was the year of the arena's opening – near one hundred years in the past.

A hundred years of blood – and now what?

It seemed that either Charlie was not on the gate or Petr's comrade kept his mouth shut, since they were – as before – waved inside the access door without challenge.

A shadow spread before them like a creeping moon, covering half the arena's floor – an enormous space filled with workmen at benches and the chaos of shouting and hammering. Men in royal livery were everywhere but Thomas noted them as vague figures only, for a steel giant dominated the centre of the arena.

It towered above those working below, scaffolding climbing several storeys like thin trees, men clinging to the sides as they measured, cut and hammered, the thump and hiss of two-man rivet guns audible over the din.

The steel giant was little more than a frame for the most part, but it still stopped Thomas in his tracks. When complete it would be a squat, beast of a war-machine, not so large as the sand-hog perhaps but more agile. The feet were complete, and most of the legs too, armoured with heavy steel plate. The body was mostly framing but it seemed to have a chair rigged up within the torso. *For the pilot.*

A clawed hand lay on the ground, each finger the size of a man as the nearest team of workman swarmed over it like ants. Copper pipes lay stacked nearby. Beside this group rested a small, cold boiler on wheels, something perhaps the size of those that powered the steam-car.

He shared what he saw with Mia until one of the guards gave Thomas a shove, starting him toward the metal giant; Petr had already crossed half the distance. Williams' man hailed a tall figure, one nonetheless still dwarfed by the machine before him. The fellow wore no hat, his dark hair free to his shoulders but he did dress in a fine suit, charcoal jacket and pants with crimson shirt sleeves peeking at the cuffs, his cane the same colour save for a black tip. A silver-handled revolver hung from his belt.

The king's eldest.

Julian.

Thomas remembered the man too well – or at least, the older boy who'd told lies about Thomas, ensuring dozens of beatings and sometimes worse. Thomas nearly reached for the thin scar beneath his eye – but Julian had turned to face them. *I'll be damned if I let him think I still care about that day.*

"Ah, Petr, I've been expecting you all morning. I trust my father didn't prattle on?"

Thomas fought to control his frown. Beside him, Mia stiffened at the sound of Julian's voice.

Petr bowed. "Certainly not, Your Highness."

"Wonderful to hear. Why don't you send one of your men into the old kitchen to check on morning tea."

Petr did so then stepped back with his remaining soldiers, creating the illusion that Thomas and Mia now spoke with Julian alone. Yet Petr watched them – it was clear that any chance for escape would not come easily.

"So. The patchling children return at last. Welcome home," Julian said, traces of the old contempt in his voice – yet now, Thomas caught something he'd always missed as a boy. Jealousy. Subtle, but something about the 'prince' suggested it, the way the derision in his voice held the casual air of nobility looking down on common-born folk, yet it did not reach the eyes – no, the man's blue eyes were bright with hatred.

Mia only folded her arms.

"Now that your father's favourite orphans have returned, you must be devastated," Thomas said, emboldened by his sudden revelation. "It's back to second fiddle, isn't it?"

Julian narrowed his eyes but did not retort. Instead, he smiled at Mia, softening his voice. "It saddens me that you cannot see the beauty of my creation, dear Mia."

"The machinery of death is not beautiful," she said.

"But it is necessary. Please, allow me to show you both some hospitality," Julian said, leaning in and taking Mia's arm. She jerked free but he took it again, steel entering his voice. "Let's not make a scene; I'd hate for someone you care about to have an accident, and this is such a dangerous worksite."

"Your father needs Thomas, you won't hurt him."

"Oh, indeed not. I need your burly brother too – no, I was referring to those here who are not as fortunate as either of you." He took her chin and turned it toward a workbench where men worked in unison to pound a sheet of steel into shape. "I know you cannot see but there are a pair of white-sands who, lately, have not been working as hard as I'd like." Next, he tilted her chin up to the great walls of the arena and Thomas followed where the man pointed, up to empty seating extending up in tiers. "And above, you will have to imagine men with magnifier-rifles, concealed but ready to shoot the moment any fool attempts escape, the moment I give the signal."

Thomas shaded his eyes against the still-rising sun, marking a single figure crouched in the space between seating, where stairs would have led down into the arena.

"For every man you see, there are two you do not," Julian told Thomas. Then he released Mia and gestured to an arched doorway some distance away. There, Fortress servants were arranging a table with three places. "Now, let's enjoy a nice meal together and I can supply some of the details my forgetful father doubtless neglected to mention – such as Thomas here being the pilot for my work of art."

Chapter 17

Rare strawberries were chill on Thomas' tongue and the wine probably the finest he would likely ever drink, but it tasted like ash – such was the lingering shock of Julian's revelation. It had been the same with the soft white bread and rich cheese. Mia was eating too, hunger outweighing her distaste for their captor, aware that Julian watched her every move over his own meal, if the way her shoulders were set was any indication.

The prince placed his silverware down upon the crimson tablecloth and leant back in his chair, wineglass in one hand – a topaz ring glittering on a finger. Again, Thomas resisted the urge to reach for the old scar beneath his eye.

"I won't pilot that thing, even if you do finish it," Thomas reiterated.

Again, Julian smiled as he replied. "It may not be completed tomorrow, but I am certainly on schedule. And you will be a fine soldier for our nation, despite your... irregular birth."

Thomas ignored the childish barb. "I will die before I kill

for you and your father."

"Really?" Julian lifted an arm, glancing over his shoulder as he did – then signalled toward the slaves working on the sheet metal.

The crack of a shot echoed in the arena.

One of the slaves crumpled to the ground without a sound. His fellows flinched and several dropped their tools. Only one looked up to the arena seating however, face drained of all colour, as the others moved to the fallen man and together, lifted and carried him toward a distant opening in the arena, low, close to the floor.

Thomas gaped.

"Shall we test my men – they haven't had a moving target for a while now. How about one of the ones taking out the fresh garbage there?"

Thomas shot to his feet, jaw clenched. "Enough."

Julian lowered his arm. "Then be a good pilot and listen while your sister stays here. We need to take a stroll." The 'prince' stood now, headed toward the giant, to the Colossus, as he called it. Thomas glanced to Mia, who nodded.

The man was gesturing with his cane. "When complete, you will be protected by two feet of steel. Your windows will be reinforced glass, impenetrable by all but diamond blade. There will be a fully circular, twelve-pound canon turret above you, and like the Gatling, all controllable from within your cockpit. The arms will bear their own steam canon too, similar to those on the sand-hog, only somewhat smaller. But unlike Elisabeth's pet, you will have three in total, and you will be far more mobile, able to break through walls and crush steam-cars even, thanks to the multiple boilers. I wish it were ready now, this is the work, the dream of two generations," he said, and now some measure of true softness entered his voice and his eyes grew distant.

He's imagining the destruction it will cause. Sick bastard. "That thing will drain an entire river to run; you have too many boilers," Thomas said.

"Not so, Thomas." The man smirked. "I have a little secret to help with that very problem, don't you worry yourself. Within a week, all will be ready for the first trial." He raised his hand to signal again, and Thomas tensed, but it was only for a team of men to bring a steel trolley over. It took four workmen to push and while none were slaves, they did not speak to the prince.

A collection of levers and dials rested on the trolley, as yet unconnected. But the levers were huge, the breadth of a man's torso. One bore a handle, little more than a grooved protrusion where, Thomas assumed, hands might grip.

Julian waved his cane. "Here are some of your tools."

"No man could use these," Thomas replied. "The weight alone—"

"It takes solid workmanship to realise this dream," Julian interrupted. "And future designs have already taken such requirements into consideration. Only someone with your... unique history can manage the Colossus, true, but have no doubt I will pilot the second Colossus myself." Some of the jealousy slipped back into the man's voice and he gripped Thomas' arm, fingers digging deep. "My father may think you and your sister are necessary but you are only a stepping stone, patchling. Remember that."

Thomas shrugged the man off. "My history?"

Julian raised an eyebrow. "You must be aware of your unusual strength? Especially when it comes to steel. It was always so, even when we were young – that is part of why Silas chose you."

Thomas fought the urge to blurt out a question – Julian would never answer. "Silas failed; I am not special."

Julian smiled. It was clear he wasn't fooled, and more, that he was happy to replace physical torment with that of withholding information. "Everything was going along swimmingly before that old fool David stole the king's property."

Thomas ignored being referred to as property. "David was no fool."

"Oh, but he was. He lacked vision; that's why he turned on us. I trust he is dead now, else you two certainly wouldn't be here."

"Do not speak of him," Thomas growled.

"Easy, Thomas. No need to look at me like that – yes, you're bigger than me now but I can still give you a thrashing any time I like and there's nothing you can do about it." He grinned. "Like the time I broke your wrist. It was in front of that base-born bitch you liked, wasn't it?"

"I don't remember," Thomas said, clenching his fists at his sides. *Don't take the bait; he'll use it as an excuse to hurt Mia. Or someone else in the arena. Stay calm. Don't take the bait.* Of course, both knew the lie for what it was but Thomas refused to acknowledge the memory, even as it battered him. The white-hot flash of pain, the way the snapping bone echoed across the square, Julian's triumphant shout and Leah's horrified expression... and all over what? That much he couldn't recall. *No doubt something trivial.*

Julian laughed but before he could continue, a cry rang out over the arena's din. The prince spun. Pale blue smoke rose from a distant workstation. Men were fleeing it, retching and coughing as they did.

More shouts echoed.

Cracking booms followed and plumes of blue smoke began to rise from all around, chaos following as soldiers ran in a dozen directions. Shots split the air too, as the riflemen shot at still unseen targets.

Julian was hollering for men. "Protect the Colossus!"

Figures clothed in powder-blue cloaks ran amongst the havoc, casting smoke bombs at soldiers and workstations alike. One spun before the Colossus to hurl a bomb at a charging group of soldiers, as he did so Thomas saw a bug-like mask on the man's face, and then the figure had slipped back into the smoke.

The prince was still screaming for men, his back to Thomas.

Use the confusion!

Thomas leapt for Julian, wrapping an arm around the man's throat and dragging back, ripping him from his feet. The cane clattered to the arena's floor. Thomas squeezed. "You're getting us out of here," he said into Julian's ear.

The prince struggled but Thomas applied more pressure. Still Julian beat at his forearm but to no avail. "I'm not letting you go until Mia and I are out of here," Thomas said as he dragged the man toward where Mia had crouched behind the table. As yet, neither soldier nor strange, cloaked figure had approached her, but she shouted for Thomas.

"I'm here," he called back.

Julian still fought but his movements were weakening when Thomas reached the table. "I have Julian," he told her. "We're leaving, stay close."

"What's happening? I smell smoke."

"Someone's attacking," Thomas replied. From behind, something crashed to the ground – it didn't seem loud enough to be parts of the Colossus. Thomas kept on, dragging the prince with him. Mia limped along nearby.

At the arched entry he stopped when a soldier burst forth, twin-shot in hand. The young man blinked when he recognised the prince, then levelled his gun at Thomas.

"I'll snap his neck," Thomas told the fellow.

The soldier hesitated. His hands trembled on the rifle. "You're already a dead man, you can't do that to a royal person."

"If he dies, so do you." Thomas tightened his grip and Julian thrashed. "All we want is to leave – we're not taking the prince with us." He dragged Julian closer to the opening, locking gazes with the soldier as he did. The man made no threatening move but he swallowed and his knuckles were white.

"Wait!" the fellow cried. "I can't let you do this – I'll shoot you if you take another step."

Thomas came to a halt, now finding himself supporting the mostly-unconscious prince. "Lad, if you shoot me, Mia will have her knife in his gut before I hit the ground. You will fail."

"Damn you."

He lowered his weapon.

Thomas pulled his hostage into the shadowy arch, taking Mia with him. Once deep enough, he paused – the soldier had run off for help. With luck, the lad would find no-one. Whoever the people in blue were, they'd keep him busy.

"Where to now?" Mia asked.

Thomas glared into the dim passage as he heaved the

unconscious prince across his shoulder. Both directions seemed exactly the same, light in the distance. No clue as to where the nearest exit lay. "We circle toward the main entry and see if it's unguarded."

He started forward, feet clapping across the stone.

"Who's attacking the machine?"

"I don't know. I've never seen anything like them – they're using that smoke and they have some sort of mask," he said. "I don't even know what's in the smoke, but it made Williams' men sick."

"Who could afford to mount such an attack?"

"Or risk it."

No answers came to mind as he hurried forth, Mia still close behind, her hand occasionally brushing against his back. So far, her leg wasn't slowing her down too much. The path was wide enough for several people abreast, which it had to be due to its old use, but Mia still kept single file with him as they had so many times before when fleeing.

The first patch of light revealed steps leading up to the first tier of seating. Thomas slowed. "I'm going to check on the arena before we go any further."

"Can we afford to stop?"

"I want to see the main entry; we may be heading into more danger if we continue toward it." He dumped the prince and took the man's revolver. *Perfect.* A dagger would have been enough but he took the gun nonetheless and placed it in Mia's hand. "Press this against his temple. If he wakes, let him know what you're holding. Same with anyone else in the passage."

"Hurry," she said.

"I will." Thomas leapt up the first few steps, then slowed

as the shouting and crashing grew louder. He peered over the last step, crawling up to set his back against the first row of stone benches.

Smoke still drifted across the arena's floor, obscuring the struggle but he saw enough. Bodies lay everywhere, most of them Julian's guard or workmen. Blue-clad shapes, too, lay motionless but many still ran in and out of the smoke. Someone who might have been Petr had liberated a mask and was leading the defence of the Colossus.

More of Williams' men were pouring into the gate, some in pairs as they wheeled small canons into the arena. Thomas ducked back down to rejoin Mia.

"We need a new plan."

She handed him the revolver, which Thomas tucked into his belt before lifting the prince again. "What about the kitchen? Someone had to prepare that meal at the arena."

"Right."

Thomas led her back toward their point of entry and this time, carried on toward the next square of light. A figure appeared ahead. The man gave a shout, an expression of shock on his face as he started to lift his rifle. Thomas dumped the prince, pulling the revolver free in almost the same motion and firing.

Gunfire echoed.

The soldier collapsed, dust motes spinning where he'd stood – like a golden ghost.

"Thomas?" Mia called his name.

"I'm fine," he said, breathing hard. He approached the soldier; the man lay face down in a pool of creeping blood. "Come on," he said as he retrieved the prince with a grunt. Someone would have heard the gunfire, even in the chaos;

they had to hurry.

The square of light was not the result of another set of steps leading up to seating, instead, a second passage lit by lamps was revealed.

He hurried within.

It led to a broad room that once might have housed training, if the weapons racks lining the walls were an indicator, but now it was a deserted kitchen. A black, potbellied stove stood against one wall and an ice-box opposite. Benches were strewn with utensils, odds and ends from fruit and other condiments. A wine rack lay broken, spilling its plum-coloured contents across the stones.

But there was a second doorway.

Thomas grabbed a lantern and pulled Mia along, then slowed for a set of stairs descending into a long corridor lined with cells. Despite the closure of the arena, the stench of old sweat and rotten hay lingered.

"Cells," Thomas said as they strode along. He adjusted the prince on his shoulder with a grunt.

"Will there be more than one way out?" Mia asked.

"I hope so."

They neared the end of the row and he slowed as he raised the lantern. Mia stumbled against him. "What is it?"

A heavy steel door gleamed in the light.

He'd chosen wrong.

"There's a door but I doubt we have the key." Once more, he dumped the prince on the ground, taking small satisfaction in the aches and bruises the man would wake with. Mia stood over him, gun poised.

"Can you break through?" Mia asked. "With your strength?"

"I don't know." He gripped the handle but it would not turn. A keyhole mocked him – he beat against the steel. A deep indentation appeared but the door did not budge. *That shouldn't be possible. The chains were one thing but this is unnatural. What did the alchemist do to me?* He levelled his shoulder and charged the door, ignoring the shockwave of pain.

The steel seemed to be buckling – but only slightly. *A serious door.*

"Did it work?"

"Not yet – I need more time."

Footsteps thundered toward them. Someone was on the stairs.

Mia swore – but it didn't seem to be at pursuit. She was rifling through Julian's clothing. The prince groaned as she worked, eyes fluttering. "We're fools," she said. "He probably has a key."

Lantern light appeared at the end of the cell block. "There!" a voice shouted.

"I've got them." Mia leapt up, reaching for the door. Thomas guided her and she began to work the key.

"Hurry," he said.

"I am – it's not turning."

"Is it even the right key?"

"I don't know. There's three of them, give me a moment."

"All right."

Thomas dragged Julian to his feet. The prince was still disoriented, struggling to regain consciousness. *Good.*

The rush of booted feet eased as a trio of soldiers neared, hesitating when they saw their prince. The young soldier from earlier was not among them.

"Stay back," Thomas commanded. He had Julian in a choke-hold once more, using the prince and his own body to shield Mia. "Sis?"

"This one fits but I can't get the sequence of turns right."

The lead soldier, a man whose sleeve was soaked with blood, pointed. "Unhand him, slave."

"Not likely." He did not glance over his shoulder. "Mia?"

"I think it's working."

Williams' soldier took a step. "Release his highness and something can be arranged, I swear it. Prince Julian is a just man."

Thomas broke into laughter. "I doubt that, friend."

"Thomas!" A grinding followed as Mia started on the door. Thomas stepped forward, giving her space.

Once the grinding stopped, Thomas grinned. "Ready?" he asked the trio. Julian was stirring, there wasn't much time.

The leader frowned. "For what?"

Thomas hurled the prince forward with all his might. The man crashed into his soldiers, sending all three tumbling to the ground, the snap of breaking bone following. Thomas spun into the opening, snatching the heavy door closed after him. A thunderous booming echoed.

Free.

Chapter 18

Thomas leant against the door a moment, eyes closed, and let the beating and muffled cursing from the other side wash over him. It was as nothing; they wouldn't open the door without the key Mia held. Even a canon would take too long.

Whenever they did break through, he planned to have Mia far, far away.

"I hear water."

Thomas opened his eyes. Mia stood before him in the lantern-light, sweat dampening her hair and the sides of her blindfold. She had cocked her head. He followed suit, and faint – beneath the sound of his breathing and the ruckus from the door – there it was. The trickle of water over stone.

"An underground stream?"

"It probably feeds the city wells," Mia said. "And you can bet Julian is using it for that thing too."

He led her along the passage, stone walls roughly cut, as their path wound down. The sound of moving water grew and the passage eventually opened into a broad cavern where a stream poured from a narrow opening in one wall, to a wide passage opposite.

A wooden rowboat sat at a tiny dock, a cold lantern hanging from its prow.

"There's a boat, Mia. It has to lead somewhere; we might just escape the city."

"And then how will we get to the southern wastes?"

He crouched by the boat, giving it a rock. "Let's figure that out once Birnhale is behind us."

"Forgive me if I start thinking now."

He chuckled. "Done."

Thomas put the lantern aside; he wanted both hands for balance – he'd never set foot inside a rowboat. He spread his hands to hover over the sides of the boat then stepped down – only to crash through into the river.

Cold water enveloped his limbs, turning his shout into a gurgle. Bubbles tinted with yellow lantern light exploded around him.

He floundered for the dock, gripping the post as his feet dislodged something. A shadow passed overhead and he kicked again, dragging himself up along the slick wood. Something snagged his boot but he broke the surface with a gasp.

"What happened?" Mia asked.

Thomas spat water. *Chilled my damn teeth.* "The boat was rotten; I fell through." He glanced over his shoulder where the rowboat was drifting away, sinking slowly. He pulled himself from the stream and something followed him, caught on his boot.

He flinched, kicking it free. Bones clattered mutely, covered in grime and the shreds of weeds.

"Mia, can you hold the lantern over the water?"

"What's wrong?"

"I just want to see something – it won't take long." He guided her to the water, then plunged in again, peering through the murk that his earlier intrusion had stirred.

Dark shapes resolved, pale patches visible. And they stretched as far as the light, and probably beyond. He reached for one, hands gripping something round. A skull, two holes for eyes. He lifted it free and sorrow washed over him, as if the skull had stored it for years and years.

But it was nothing so fanciful. *I know who this is – who all of them are.*

He released the skull and surfaced.

"All right, what is it?" Mia asked as he pulled himself into the dock once again.

"Bodies. Dozens of them – maybe more."

"Whose?"

"I can only guess... but I think it's all the slaves who the city was told had won their freedom."

"Oh..." Her voice softened. "We can't know that for sure."

"I know, but it makes sense. Who *ever* heard anything about a single champion after they won? And this passage right near the cells? You know what Williams and his family is like."

"I hope you're wrong but I doubt it."

He sighed. "Well, either way I think we have to swim. Can you manage? I think I can use my shirt to tie us together."

"It hasn't been *that* long since we swam the Royal Lake; just hold my hand, the water doesn't sound too fast. Do you need the lantern?"

"I don't think I have a choice." He rested a hand atop it a

moment. "I can't carry it and swim."

"The river has to lead somewhere. Otherwise there'd be no boat."

"True, but how far is that somewhere?"

"We have to find out." Thomas slid back into the stream and began treading water, raising his arms for Mia. "Sit on the edge and I'll help you in."

Mia did so, hissing when she hit the cold water, but he was able to grip her hand and together, they swam into the current. It was difficult at first, to kick and use their arms together but they soon settled into a rhythm, and the lantern light faded behind them.

Their splashing was the only sound in the blackness, but the current pulled them along steadily. Thomas soon lost track of time but the total darkness did not last. A faint glow appeared ahead, pale like sunlight rather than the warmer tone of lamplight.

"We're getting close to the end," Thomas said.

When they swam into the light, Thomas squinted – sun blind – but the sky soon resolved, along with almost barren banks sliding by. They were passing through low canyon walls, and here, the few trees that grew seemed green and healthy. When he glanced over his shoulder, the city was not as far behind as he'd hoped – the haze of steam and smog was too close.

Yet, they had to make use of the head start – for Julian would be on their trail soon enough; the man would know of the stream and where it led.

"Let's head ashore." He angled toward the bank, his eye on a small cluster of trees, their lowest branches within reach. Mia kicked with him but before they drew near, a blue-clad figure stepped from behind the trees. He reached out a hand. A black hourglass stood clear against the skin of his wrist. The man wore no mask but a hood concealed half of his face, revealing only unshaven cheeks and a smile. "Grab hold."

Thomas caught one of the branches and pushed Mia up to the man, then climbed free himself. Thomas went to Mia immediately, but the stranger made no threatening move though he was armed with a bone-handled revolver. The weapon Thomas had stolen from Julian was probably useless for now, if the powder was wet.

"You two certainly made your mark on the place. Shame you didn't kill that bastard Julian though," the man said.

Beside him, Mia's posture relaxed a little. *Maybe she feels something about him; too bad I can't ask her yet.* Which meant the stranger would still have to be watched, despite the appearance of common goals.

"You and your men made quite a stir yourselves," Thomas replied.

"A first step only," he replied. His tone darkened. "And a costly one – we've done some damage and set back the construction of the Colossus but too many died for such small gains."

"How big is your force?" Mia asked.

He paused. "Perhaps I should ask a little more about you both – and introduce myself too. I'm Ethan, leader of a rebel force here in Birnhale." He pushed his hood back to reveal a determined expression and green eyes beneath sandy blonde hair. A large bruise covered his cheek but he still smiled. "How did you come to be Julian's prisoners?"

Thomas looked to Mia, who still did not offer much in

the way of concern with her body language, her face or her voice as she shared the very basics of their story. "We should thank you and your men," she finished. "Williams has plans for us and you have thwarted them for now."

Ethan raised an eyebrow. "You are twice escaped; I am impressed. And Julian obviously thought he had you in the palm of his hand."

"He wants me to pilot the Colossus; something I will never do," Thomas said.

"I see." He nodded, as if deciding something for himself. "To answer your earlier question; our force is not nearly big enough. But it will grow as word spreads. People will flock to us now."

"Because of the attack?"

"Partially," the man replied. "But there's more. I can show you, if you wish."

Thomas glanced once more to Mia, who did not answer, though she appeared thoughtful. Despite the man's seeming good nature and good cause, and even the sense of debt that Thomas had to admit he felt, joining a band of rebels was not the wisest choice. "Our path may lie in a different direction. I'm sorry."

Ethan nodded. "I see. It is a difficult choice, not one every man can make."

Thomas frowned. "I have to think of my sister. Her safety comes before any futile rebellion, no matter how well-intentioned."

He spread his hands. "I apologise; it's not my place to judge you. If you will trust me, I can offer you both shelter and supplies for wherever it is you plan to travel – even transportation, without both of which you will doubtless perish or be caught." He paused. "You know I do not need to lie about this. The lands to the south are inhospitable and the north is naught but desert and death. To the west the Inland Federation will turn you away. You have little choice."

Mia folded her arms now. "And what do you ask in return?"

"All you have to do is help us with the second strike – we're ambushing Williams' supply train at dawn two days hence, and we'll take all the help we can. What do you say?"

"You're offering provisions and transportation?" Mia asked.

"A steam-car, good for as long as the roads last," he said.

Mia turned to look up at Thomas. "Do we have a choice?"

He sighed. Some help would be welcome. And their provisions and possessions were still in the palace. If Ethan was as genuine as he seemed... "If we don't, we strike out alone, with no supplies and on foot."

She turned back to Ethan's direction. "Very well, Ethan. You have a deal – the help of two escaped slaves, one blind and the other exhausted."

Ethan clapped his hands together, a grin lighting his face. "Good. Follow me then, the camp is not too far."

Chapter 19

The rebel camp had been tucked away in a depression at the top of a canyon, guarded on all sides by men with magnifier-rifles – these fellows dressed in tan to blend with the surrounding stone. Ethan assured them there was a second exit, one other than the path he led them up.

At the top, wind skimmed over the stone above, penetrating the camp and stirring tent-flaps. From Thomas' vantage point at the crest, nothing looked so permanent that it couldn't be broken down and moved in less than half an hour – save perhaps the steam-canon facing the crest.

Men and women both moved about the camp, and most activity centred around a large cauldron. Many were still clad in blue, fresh bandages visible, while others wore the tan. *There has to be a hundred at least.* More than he'd expected but hardly enough to overthrow a Kingdom. *Or break years and years of deeply-entrenched slavery.*

The scent of chicken and spice crossed the camp. It seemed to draw Ethan in, as he quickened his step, waving for them to follow. Thomas helped Mia along the uneven ground, past the small tents and the sombre faces. The camp was quiet, despite the queues at the cauldron, and most people only gave them passing glances. Were they thinking about those who'd died in the attack? Or about the danger to come? *Those who died would have preferred to die free than to live in chains, surely.* He'd only been re-enslaved for a few days but he knew he could never go back to that life.

And yet, Mia didn't need a dead martyr.

He had to live to protect her; even if that meant a chance of being a slave once more. *It's that simple.*

Ethan took them to a large tent and held the flap open. "I'll bring some food soon. Sit and take some water if you will." The rebel leader reached out a hand to assist Mia to some cushions. "My lady."

"You're kind to offer but I'm fine, Ethan," Mia said, no resentment in her voice. In fact, she seemed pleased that he'd offered and accepted his help.

"Of course." He turned back to the camp.

Thomas slumped beside Mia. The cushions were dry and his clothing was still damp but he hoped Ethan wouldn't mind. After a moment, Thomas groaned and stretched for a small table, filling mugs from a pitcher. The tent was sparsely furnished. No cot; no chest – just an old pack, probably Ethan's own. A lamp hung from the ceiling, illuminating maps and plans pinned to the canvas.

"Mia?"

"Yes?" Her voice was not as weary as he'd expected.

"Do you feel anything? About Ethan and his plans, I mean."

She nodded slowly, a slight frown touching her brow. "Yes. Noble intentions. I feel safe here, I'm surprised to admit."

"Then we're not in danger?"

"We're always in danger, aren't we?"

"Sadly, yes."

"Well, that danger comes from elsewhere, not Ethan and his rebels." She paused to drink, holding the mug after she finished, tapping her fingers on it – revealing cuts and scrapes doubtless earned during their escape. "I see him standing before us, blazing brand in hand – protecting us from a shadow of pitch. He's holding it back." Her voice had softened as she spoke.

Thomas raised his eyebrows. "That's a clear image, isn't it?"

"So far."

The canvas door rustled as Ethan returned, two blue-clad figures in tow.

One was a short woman, her hair caught in a long braid, tied with strands of copper. *An expensive accessory.* Yet her face was weary and her clothing worn; nowhere else did she sport such ornamentation. The second fellow was an older man with greying dreadlocks, his expression one of open hope as he followed Ethan inside.

"This is Genevieve and Carlo," Ethan said. "They are my seconds, if you will."

Thomas introduced himself after Mia had done so, receiving nods, before asking Ethan about the raid. "How can we help?"

"You may find it odd but I have been made... aware of your family's talents, Thomas. Forgive me for not revealing this earlier."

Thomas frowned. *Another person who seems to know us better than we know ourselves.* Had Mia been mistaken about the man? Yet she did not react to his admission. "How?"

"Our benefactor is well-connected in the Fortress." He raised a hand, as if to forestall any further questions. "It is best for all that I do not reveal their identity at this point."

Thomas folded his arms, ready to push the point but Mia spoke first.

"What did Silas tell you about us?"

Genevieve had shifted her feet and Ethan raised an eyebrow, only to chuckle. He seemed impressed. "Well, I shouldn't be surprised. He said you would be able to offer keen insight, even foresight, and that your brother bore an unusual affinity for working with steel." Even though Mia could not see it, Ethan smiled at her. "It's my hope that you can help us with the raid, by at the least warning us now if we are doomed."

Mia shook her head. "I see no failure for your raid for now. That is all he said?"

"We rarely have time to speak as I'd wish."

Genevieve sighed. "We're all tired, Ethan. Let's just brief them so we can get some rest. Tomorrow will be a long day."

"You're right about that." Ethan moved to the maps, pointing to a road marked north of the city. It wound down through the hills, eventually reaching Birnhale. "Here is the northern highway, connecting the Last Farms of Birnhale to the capital. Since our last attack on the mines, the King will attempt to sneak copper for the Colossus in with the produce." He shifted his finger, still some distance from the city. "We'll strike here. We need to deny them the copper, even if it means destroying it."

"And is that where I come in?" Thomas asked.

"Perhaps," Ethan said. "The copper is usually stored in steel crates, difficult to break into during a raid, difficult to transport. We don't need to open the crates to prevent Williams getting his hands on the contents, but having you ready would be of comfort."

"Are you sure of all this?"

"Alchemist said so himself," Carlo said, his voice quiet. "You can trust his word."

"Can I?"

"He's been working on this rebellion for years," Ethan added. "It would be a strange time to betray everyone."

Thomas frowned. *Just what are we caught up in now?* Silas was pulling strings from afar, it seemed. The Alchemist would have answers, that much was clear. *We need to speak to him. Or get Ethan to reveal whatever he knows.* "I'll do my best."

Ethan slapped him on the shoulder. "Good man. Why don't we eat and get some rest. If you have no more questions?"

"Just one. Did Silas tell you we'd be at the arena earlier?"

"He did. We hoped to find you of course, but the main objective was to disrupt the construction of the Colossus." Ethan gestured to the camp beyond the tent. "I know you seek answers and perhaps I hold some, but save the rest of your questions until after the meal – I hate to let good food grow cold."

Chapter 20

In the end, it was hard to find a reason not to help Ethan and his band of rebels.

Aside from Mia.

Thomas sighed as he followed Ethan across a busy market square in Birnhale, the sun harsh upon his back and the humid air from the not-too distant river combining for an unpleasant walk. Worse was the hood he wore – but it was part of a necessary disguise. Even though Mia had assured Thomas there was little to fear, that she would be safe in the camp and he would be safe in the city, he couldn't shake the sensation of eyes boring into him. Yet whenever he glanced around the square or up to windows and dark rooves, he caught no hint of movement from any watcher.

Of course, Williams' men were no doubt searching but so far, he'd seen no-one and seemed to draw no attention. He and Ethan were dressed as factory workers in worn overalls beneath their cloaks, Thomas with his hood and Ethan wearing a wide-brimmed hat common enough in the city.

"This is the merchant," Ethan said when he paused before

a storefront, its windows filled with colourful displays of fine fabrics. The slender blue dress alone, its sleeves lined in sequins, would have cost enough to feed an entire family in the Hungry Quarter. *Ten years ago, Mia might have been the one to sew the sequins.*

"A dressmaker is your contact with Silas?"

"More like our funnel."

"For what?"

"Funding." Ethan pushed on the door before Thomas could ask more about the Alchemist. A bell rang as they stepped through. Thomas joined him in a narrow room where a counter blocked access to more clothing, mostly dark suits but also fanciful hats with feathers and glass jewels on display. Near the window, two chairs stood empty.

An older man glanced up over his spectacles from where he wrote in a ledger. "I'm sorry gentlemen but if you're looking for a seamstress to repair your garments, you'll have to try the harbour, we have no room for..." he trailed off, squinting. "Ethan?"

"Of course." Ethan removed his hat.

"You're a little late – I was going to send word," the old man said, a hint of disapproval in his voice, which was now at least a shade warmer than it had been when he thought they were 'mere' factory workers.

"No need to trouble yourself," Ethan replied. He made no effort to introduce Thomas, nor did Thomas volunteer. Thankfully, the dressmaker did not seem inclined to ask.

The fellow nodded, placing his quill aside – then moved between the rows of clothing and into an adjoining room. He soon returned, carrying a head-sized hessian bag, which he tossed to Ethan.

"Swiftly now, Ethan – I don't like attention on my shop."

"I know the drill, Francis."

When they returned to the market, Thomas followed Ethan through the cobbled streets, drawing nearer the harbour until the buildings began to change. Not quite so poor as the Hungry Quarter; the brickwork was just as sturdy but the timber of upper stories was more often stained with soot, the thud and clank of steelworks provided a constant undercurrent and the people they passed wore dark expressions, many bearing the hourglass, some with overseers prodding them along.

A cat slunk across the path before them; it was missing an ear, its fur mottled.

"Who's buying fine goods from the Royal Market here?" Thomas asked. The hessian bag didn't seem heavy enough to contain gold or silver.

Ethan's mouth tightened into a thin line. "Misery is for sale everywhere – people will always find a way to afford more."

Thomas didn't ask the next question; it was clear he wouldn't like the answer. Whatever the contents were, he had to find a way to overlook. Ethan seemed a good enough fellow, and he was committed to the end of slavery – that was a worthy pursuit. Whatever else he did, the man would have to answer for in whatever afterlife awaited him.

The next building they approached housed no merchant or even furniture – it was little more than a shack built up against a tavern, standing amongst a withered garden. Thorn bushes that looked to have borne no rose for years were turning white.

Within, a street urchin crouched beyond a shaft of

light that slipped between missing tiles in the roof. He straightened at the sight of them; body tensed, ready for flight, but smiled when Ethan removed his hat.

"Finally!"

"I know, I know," Ethan said. "I'm late. Tell her I'm here."

The lad made no effort to leave, scratching at matted hair. "Who's your friend?"

"No-one you need to be concerned about, Boots. Just get moving – I don't want her to take it out on you."

"She'd have to catch me first," the lad said, then slipped from the shack via a door at the rear.

"Who are we waiting for?" Thomas asked.

Ethan dumped the hessian sack at his feet and leant against a solid-seeming part of the wall. "Lina. She's dependable in her own fashion and we need her money."

"You don't trust her."

"Not beyond the bounds of our transaction, no. But she knows that if anything happens to me, she cuts off her supply."

Thomas frowned at the hessian sack. There was little doubt now as to what had been smuggled via the dressmaker. Star-dust. When he was younger he'd thought it similar to opium's euphoric effects but it gave a dangerous rush before the more pleasant sedation kicked in. Long term-users became violent monsters, making it much worse than opium.

And Lina would be the powder-rat who sold it.

When she finally breezed into the shack, it was with two heavily-armed men in tow, one of which carried a small chest. Lina herself had once been beautiful – dark eyes and full red lips marred by papery skin and a gaping hole where her nostrils once connected to the top of her lip.

Thomas fought back a shudder.

Like a walking corpse.

Yet cunning lurked beneath the slight haze that ghosted across her eyes as she regarded them both, hands on hips. She wore men's pants and a leather corset; bare arms revealed twin hourglasses, one of black and the other yellow. Neither man spoke while she appraised Ethan.

"I don't like to wait, Rebel," she said, her tone frost-laden.

"But you will, won't you?" Ethan replied, his own voice bearing little but distaste. He bent to lift the hessian sack. "You can't say no to star-dust this pure and we both know it."

Lina rolled her eyes. "Finished with your little power-play?"

Ethan tossed the sack to the empty-handed man, who caught it and immediately set it down to untie the drawstring. The crinkle of waxed paper followed as he looked within, then nodded up to Lina.

"Pay him," she said.

The fellow with the chest looked to Thomas. Ethan gestured for him to cross the space between them. Thomas did so and accepted the chest; it was heavy but nothing he couldn't manage. Before he could turn, Lina stepped closer to peer at him. The scent of lavender and something else washed over him.

"And who are you, then? New muscle?"

"Exactly," he said, and re-joined Ethan before she could touch him.

"Until next month," she said with a smile.

Ethan did not answer, turning on his heel instead.

Thomas followed him outside and along the nearest street, turning down an alley and heading back toward the richer parts of Birnhale. At an intersection he stopped, letting a steam-car rattle up the hill. A crimson flag flew from the carriage.

"I know what you're thinking," Ethan said as they waited.

"Do you?"

"Yes. You think I should get my money elsewhere."

Thomas shrugged. "Perhaps, but I still appreciate what you're trying to do."

"I'm glad to hear that," he said, glancing to Thomas. "We'll be in your debt, you know. All of us. And especially Silas."

"Why Silas?"

"He risked a lot, helping you escape the palace. There was another man, I believe – David?"

"Yes," Thomas said absently but he missed Ethan's next words. *Silas helped us escape, why?* What did the man gain by doing so? And if it was to help the rebels... what would that achieve? Did the Alchemist have an eye on the Kingdom? "Why?"

"It's not my place, to be honest," Ethan replied. Then he shook his head at himself. "I'll give you my own opinion though; I think guilt might be a motivator."

Thomas frowned. "For what he did to me?"

"Yes."

"And what was that exactly?"

"I don't know; Silas doesn't share his experiments but I know that not all of them are successful."

A shout rang across the street before Thomas could ask another question.

Soldiers were dragging a thin man from a nearby home. One knocked a potted plant from the window box with his elbow, the pottery shattering, spraying dirt across the street. "You've had your last chance," another of Williams' men snapped.

The thin fellow continued to thrash and a woman with a bleeding lip charged out of the house, beating at one of the soldiers. "Leave us be!"

The soldier ignored her. His fellow, the man who held their charge, spoke over her cries. "Alfred Manus, you are now the property of the King, due at the Fortress for assignment. You will come willingly or unconscious. Choose."

Thomas had already taken a step when Ethan caught his arm, the man's grip like iron. "Don't."

"We can stop this," Thomas said. His jaw ached from clenching his teeth.

"No," Ethan said, his voice pitched low. "If we intervene we lose the money – I can't afford that. I need the weapons and the medicine it will buy. More, you'll give yourself away. Those soldiers will have descriptions of you."

"Dead men tell no tales, Ethan."

"And what good are you to Mia if you're caught?"

Thomas hissed. *Damn it, he's right.* "Fine."

"This way. The others are waiting."

By the time they reached the sprawling grounds of the armoury where it perched atop the lesser hill before the Fortress, Thomas had cooled off, though the woman's cries of anguish echoed. *Somehow, I'd forgotten that sound.*

But there was little time to dwell on it, Ethan had completed his transformation. He now wore a dark blue suit with black gloves, a bowler hat – and had even pinned a sprig of rosemary to his lapel.

"A new custom," Ethan explained before opening the heavy, steel door.

Inside, the walls were covered with steel plating, stout windows cloaked in steel mesh. Rifles and revolvers lined the walls, along with canon barrels. Ammunition rested in boxes on the many shelves, the sharp points of the willow-shot standing like miniature palisades.

A heavy-set Bruiser wearing the serpent of a Captain's insignia on his flak jacket approached, taking Ethan's hand. "Lord Pryor, you are looking well."

"I certainly feel well, Wade," Ethan replied, affecting a nasal voice. He even stood differently, hands clasped behind his back. He looked to the nearest rack of rifles. "I assume you had enough magnifiers and twin-shot?"

The Bruiser bowed. "All is ready – we're finishing up loading your steam-car as we speak."

"Grand. My porter will pay you."

Wade nodded before grunting at Thomas and jerking a finger over his shoulder toward a small doorway. Thomas carried the chest to the door. No-one was present, so he knocked.

The door opened and a bearded man raised an eyebrow. "Yes?"

"Lord Pryor's account."

"Set it down in here."

Thomas entered a bare room and sat the chest on a steel table before turning for the door. "Wait," the man said without looking up from where he was already counting out coins.

"Is there a problem?" Thomas kept his voice steady, despite the stab of concern. Had Lina betrayed them after all?

"Your change." The fellow handed over a heavy purse, perhaps a tenth of the money in the chest. "Take it directly to his lordship, slave."

"Yes." *I'd rather shove it down your throat.*

But he returned to 'Lord Pryor' who had finished with the Bruiser and was even now waving Thomas toward another doorway. This admitted them into a narrow corridor lined with doors, all concealing the muffled sounds of workshops. Beyond the passage waited a large staging area with men carrying a few final wooden boxes to a hissing steam-car.

Carlo sat in the driver's seat and two more of the rebels, each dressed as Thomas, helped the armoury soldiers with the final boxes, stacking them in a trailer. Ethan motioned for Thomas to join them, where he helped one of the rebels tie a canvas cover over the goods and then he was climbing into the car.

"Onward, driver."

The steam-car started slowly but soon picked up speed as it followed the curve of the hill around and away from the armoury. Large mansions with high walls stood beyond the road. Many boasted large but greying gardens before the walls. *So only the Fortress stays green, it seems.*

"Well done, everyone," Ethan said with a smile.

Thomas found himself unable to join the rebel leader – as up ahead, a steam car appeared, blocking the road. Half a dozen soldiers stood before the vehicle. They carried twin-shots and while their faces were too distant to make out, Thomas imagined grim expressions.

"Trouble ahead," Carlo said.

Ethan's smile faded. "Stick to the story; this could be routine, nothing more."

"And if it isn't?" Thomas asked. "If they're looking for me – or if they know Lord Pryor is a ruse? Or maybe they're just on alert after your attack."

"Then get ready to follow my lead."

"What does that mean?"

Ethan grinned. "It means I'm going to make it up as I go."

Chapter 21

Thomas gripped the revolver, keeping it beneath his clothing where he sat, waiting for Carlo to bring the steam-car to a halt. The nearest fellow raised a hand, approaching the passenger seat, where Ethan sat directly before Thomas. He glanced out the window – if he had to run, was there any cover near the homes... the sun glinted on steel atop one of the walls. A magnifier rifleman – no escape that way.

"Something wrong, Sergeant?" Ethan asked. His voice was nasal once more but calm enough, carrying some annoyance – just like the spoilt nobleman he was pretending to be.

"Just increasing security, my lord," the lead man said. He swallowed and opened his mouth, unable to speak at first. "As, ah, part of the King's new measures we've started searching all weapons leaving the armoury... and we're also required to confirm your identity."

"I see." A deep disapproval had crept into Ethan's voice. "And just how do you propose to do that?"

Thomas gripped his gun; if the sergeant saw Ethan's tattoo...

"Well… Forgive me, but there is a way and it won't detain you for but a moment."

Ethan leant across the window. "Then do so and let me be on my way."

"Yes, my lord. If you could just remove your glove and roll up your sleeve."

Ethan glared at the soldier before tugging at the fingers of his gloves, tossing the glove into Carlo's lap. Then he rolled his sleeve up and lifted his wrist. "Satisfied?"

Thomas held his breath. Surely the man would see…

But the poor soldier barely glanced at Ethan's skin before thanking the 'lord', calling off the search and waving for his own driver to move their car, unblocking the road. Ethan sat back, snapping at Carlo to resume driving.

Williams' men were soon well behind them, the climbing hills of Birnhale's outskirts soon rising, bird calls growing where before it had been the rumble of the city. The change in air was welcome too, cleaner, almost sweet in comparison.

"How did he miss your tattoo?" Thomas asked.

Ethan lifted his arm once more, this time with a grin. The tattoo was gone – only smooth, clear skin remained on his wrist.

"No-one could erase the hourglass so perfectly…"

"I'm not convinced of that but this is only paint," Ethan said with a chuckle.

"But the match is amazing," Thomas said. He could not tell where natural skin began and paint ended.

"Practice makes perfect."

"Impressive." Thomas leant into his seat and rubbed at the back of his neck, easing some of the tension. Despite Mia's assurance that he'd be safe, it had been a little too easy to forget her words when confronted with half a dozen twin-shots.

By the time the car reached a fork in a road, the afternoon was wearing on. Yet the supplies had to be taken up into the hills and the lingering light wasn't going to make the job easier. Ethan sent his men about their business, as though they'd had everything planned well in advance. *And no doubt they have.* Men with magnifier rifles were sent to positions either end of the road, carrying small hand mirrors to signal.

Other men, well over a score, had poured down from the hills and even now they were forming lines and passing weapons, ammunition and medicine into the hills, up the narrow path that would lead to the camp.

Once the car was emptied, Carlo drove it north, where he would stage a breakdown to delay any other drivers. If none appeared, he would hide the car in its cave before covering his tracks. As for the path leading back to the city, Ethan had a much more dramatic method.

He produced a store of gunpowder, hidden within a small chest. "I fire this and make a hole in the road; that would be all the advance warning we need, whether it's Williams or a pack of nobles out for pleasure rides."

"And if it's a troop of soldiers on foot?"

Ethan's expression hardened. "Then we shoot every last one and hide the bodies."

Thomas offered a slow nod. It was probably the only way to be certain, even though it seemed brutal, if necessary. "The explosion will draw too much attention; Julian might change his path or even the day."

"I know. It's a last resort," Ethan said. "And we'll be swift – help them now and we'll be back in the camp in no time."

Thomas joined the rebels, carrying his share up into the hills. At regular intervals he handed his store of weapons to another man and trekked back down to take a new bundle from the fellow behind him. Quicker than he'd expected – even with Ethan's assurance – the work was done and Thomas found himself heading for Ethan's tent.

Mia waited within, head over a steaming bowl of soup. By its colour he guessed it was tomato – something he hadn't eaten in years. "I hope there's some of that left," he said.

"There should be," she said with a smile. "Everything went according to plan?"

He grinned. "You don't know?"

"Just a feeling; no details this time."

"It went well enough." Thomas explained the day's events. He still wasn't sure what to make of being one of Silas' 'experiments'. Anger that he hadn't realised still lingered now slipped into his voice – fuelled in part by everything he saw in the city, the drugs and the enslavement too – but Mia took and squeezed his hand. "You're still my brother, no matter what."

Some of his anger slipped away. "Thank you."

"I find it hard to believe Ethan's involved with spreading star-dust," Mia said after a moment's silence. She sounded quite disappointed.

"He doesn't like it."

"At least he'll put the weapons to good use. I know that much," Mia said.

"You've seen something?"

Mia nodded. "Yes but I don't know what to make of it. This is more than a feeling, this time. I see two paths. In one, you and I are heading south and in the other, we're back in the city."

Thomas frowned as his stomach flipped. "As slaves?"

"Yes."

"But you see Ethan putting a stop to Julian's train?"

"It's a slaughter," she whispered. "Many are going to die, and not just the king's men. People here too. It hangs on a needle's thread."

Thomas hesitated. "Do you... see it? The dead, I mean – or is it a feeling like during other times?"

"This time I see it," she said, a trace of sadness in her voice. "But I'm not squeamish so you don't have to worry." He placed his other hand over hers, and but she pulled her own hand away, giving his a pat. "I meant what I said, Thomas. Don't be concerned."

"All right. What of your doubt?"

The tent flap rustled and Ethan entered, holding two bowls of steaming soup. "Good evening. I've brought the last of our tomatoes," Ethan said, handing one of the tin bowls to Thomas with a smile. He turned to Mia. "Ah, I see you've eaten, Mia."

"I have, but thank you for the gesture," she said. "I'm impressed that the rebel leader himself would serve us." Her voice contained a trace of a smile.

"Old habits," Ethan said with a chuckle and his gaze lingered on her. "No matter how long I am free I find these odd reminders of my time bearing the black."

She nodded. "It's impossible to forget."

Thomas had already inhaled half his soup, the saltiness a welcome explosion of flavour. Even half-distracted as he was by the meal, he noted Ethan's hesitance. And what seemed like an interest in Mia, one that she might have returned?

He couldn't be sure.

Nor did he know quite how to feel about it either, if he was right.

"I wanted to ask if you've seen anything about tomorrow?" Ethan asked.

"Many will die," Mia said. "But there's a chance you will succeed, yes."

He sighed. "Not as heartening as I'd hoped. But we have no choice. Thank you, Mia. I'd better get this soup to Jonas. Sleep well, the both of you," he said as he left.

Thomas finished his meal and set the bowl aside. He nearly asked her about Ethan but said instead, "Do you sense anything else about tomorrow?"

"About the two paths?" She shook her head. "It's worse than that rat in the suit; it makes even less sense. I see a pocket watch with a moon face – and it's important somehow, that's all I know."

Thomas exhaled. "Well, it's better than nothing. Is there a time on the face? It might be the time to strike?"

"No, the hands are set to twelve but it's the object that's important, not a time of day or night. I sense that much, as strongly as I ever have."

"All right. I'll watch for a timepiece set with a moon and everything will be fine."

"By tomorrow we'll know for certain," she said, her smile difficult to read. Did she mean for it to bolster his spirits, or her own? He could not bring himself to ask.

Chapter 22

Saint's Bridge was a narrow span of steel that crossed a ravine, a river thundering below. The rush of the current was like a constant angry murmur. It didn't look so high, but without the bridge no steam-cars or carriages were getting across the ravine. They could head miles and miles out of their way and approach Birnhale via the east but the bridge was quicker.

And the perfect place for Ethan's ambush.

"Collapse the bridge and let the river swallow them up – it's that simple," he'd said before leading the force out of the camp in the cool pre-dawn.

Thomas had once again left Mia in the care of those who stayed behind, extracting a promise that she would flee with the others if he didn't return that evening. She hadn't wanted to agree, he knew, but she'd still said the words that would send him forth, the words that would give them the best chance for escape.

Now Thomas and Ethan were crouched in the hills above their target, staring down on the bridge, watching the rising sun glint upon its steel arches like a slow-creeping flame. The clicks and snaps of rifles being loaded and checked over filled the quiet – the tan-clothed rebels setting up positions behind stunted trees or large stone protrusions.

"Are you sure of Silas' information?" Thomas asked.

Ethan slapped Thomas on the back. "He hasn't been wrong once. In fact, I'd wager if you take a look you'll see Julian's train approaching now." Ethan motioned for the nearest man to lend the magnifier rifle.

Thomas gripped the weapon. It was far heavier than the willow-rifles – the chamber held a much longer bullet too – but most of the weight came from the adjustable lens. It was mounted in such a way that if he looked through to his target – the bridge – it grew much closer, although the edges of his view were distorted. When he twisted the dial, the scene neared a second time, enough to make out the pebbles beyond the bridge.

Had a man been in his sights, the shot would have been quite possible – almost easy.

And there was movement on the other side of the span. A steam car approached, mostly a dark shadow until it fully crested a rise. It towed a carriage, which was in turn, followed by another car. Three in total, and scores of soldiers supporting – they clung to the sides and rooves, some with rifles held ready. More men seemed to follow, their shapes far less distinct.

Julian would be waiting somewhere in the van but Thomas didn't dare attempt a shot, tempting though it was.

Ethan's plan relied on Julian leading his men halfway across the bridge, then pinning them under heavy fire while he and Thomas attempted to sabotage the structure. A madman's run he called it, and there was a glint in his eye when he spoke. *Damn fool's looking forward to it.*

"They're approaching," Thomas said as he returned the rifle.

"Good. Ready?"

Thomas nodded. Ethan signalled to his men and started down the crooked path. The road waited below, empty, draped in a hush for the moment. Mia's words followed Thomas' every step. *It's going to be a slaughter.*

"I get the feeling that Silas has been planning something like this for some time," Thomas said.

"He has," Ethan replied. "Not this precisely, but something like it."

"He's been quick to take advantage of my and Mia's talents. Maybe not a surprise, since he's the one responsible for my... skills."

Ethan nodded. "After this, I'm expecting him to call another meeting. I know he's most keen to talk with you and your sister. I suspect he'll ask you to stay on and support us in our efforts." He held up a hand as they continued their descent. "And before you say you have to think of Mia, I know that but I think toppling Williams is the best way to do so."

"Not if she dies in the struggle," Thomas said, detouring a gouge in the path. He couldn't deny wanting to finally speak with the alchemist himself but escaping to the south was still more important. *Right after surviving this anyway.*

"We all die."

"It doesn't have to be soon though."

Ethan laughed. "Have a little faith, Thomas."

The path met broken ground before the road, where they

paused behind a wind-worn boulder. "We won't have much time – we need them at least in the centre before we start."

"Are you sure I can do this?" Thomas asked. Snapping chains and beating down doors was one thing but collapsing a bridge? *Maybe I am unique but I'm not that unique.*

"Silas knows his business. I've checked the bridge myself; it's older than it looks. If you can break the supports in exactly the right spot, the weight of three steam cars and all that copper and the men will be enough to dump everything into the river."

"And how do we avoid the same fate?"

Ethan produced a coil of rope from his belt. "You'll be tied to me; I can pull you to safety." He pointed. "See that bolt, driven into the earth? It's the anchor."

Thomas sighed. "This is a big risk. You'll be out in the open."

"I know." His expression didn't change from one of determination. "But I'll have cover from above. And I'll have you."

Once again, Thomas was reminded just how specifically this plan had been designed for his particular skills. What was Silas up to? *And exactly what did the alchemist do to me all those years ago? Why can't I remember?*

"Fine. Let me tie my waist now then," Thomas said, taking the heavy coil. "I'll throw you your end before I climb out."

"Right."

The first steam car rumbled onto the bridge – still a good fifty yards away but Thomas gripped the rope harder. Once all three were on the bridge... he kept his eyes on the lead car. *He couldn't forget Mia's vision either.* "Ethan, do you own a timepiece?"

"I did. Why?"

"Was there a moon on the face?"

"No. Did Mia see something?"

"She said our success depends on my finding it during the attack." Which wasn't entirely true but nor was it a lie. Her vision suggested success for she and Thomas. Would Ethan survive the slaughter? Carlo? Genevieve?

"Is it a symbol?"

"She's certain it's an object."

Ethan rubbed at the stubble on his jaw. "Well, nothing we can do but keep an eye out for it. The bridge first. And it's about time, ready?"

The third car was on the bridge now. "I guess I have to be."

Thomas dashed to the road and then ran at a crouch, heart thumping. Was a rifle round about to knock him from his feet? The lead car was still approaching, driving slowly across the narrow span, obscured by its arches. Ethan's boots pounded along behind him.

At the bridge he skidded to a halt, stirring dust, before tossing the rope back to Ethan. Then he swung down to grip the ladder – right where Ethan had said it would lie – and began climbing down. He quickly reached the support, stretching out across the river, vibrations from the cars thrumming through his grip.

The Saint's River was a dark mass below. If he fell and Ethan's rope failed, he'd not die from the fall itself, but who knew where the strong current would take him? Or what rocks lay submerged waiting to dash him to pieces.

Surrounded by steel, his body began to respond. A flicker in his chest, and warmth spread across his torso, radiating down his limbs, and tickling at his fingertips. It built, churning within. Not disconcerting but almost *right,* yet that made little sense. His very skin seemed to steam – though that was a trick of his mind, surely. Even his mind seemed infused with heat. There was comfort in it, a familiarity, but there was no fear. *Why? Why doesn't this scare me?*

He had little time to contemplate. When he reached near the limit of his rope, he glanced back at Ethan, barely visible, crouching by the pole.

Gunfire rang out.

Bullets ricocheted against steel and shouts rose from the supply lines. Orders were roared and the gunfire continued. Thomas flinched when steel screeched against steel, rocking the very bridge. He kept moving while the answering crack of rifles returned fire on the hills. Men cried out and others swore; Julian's voice rose above it all, harrying his force.

But it seemed to be working, the line had stopped, forced to take cover no doubt.

Thomas found the beams; they'd been marked with a slash of red paint.

Shaking his head, Thomas slammed the heel of his palm into the bridge. A boom followed and he nearly lost his grip. The whole bridge had vibrated and his hand barely registered the impact. He struck again and a third time. The steel was giving way, bowing. Grinding sounds followed – the bridge was holding but if he kept it up, it might just work.

The sense of triumph faded quickly.

He'd still have to either leap into the river and hope Ethan was able to pull him out, or strike the bridge enough so that it *nearly* collapsed, giving himself time to turn back, before it fell into the water. Was it even possible? *Have I made a mistake?* Too late to turn back – he had to keep going, everyone depended on him. Mia, Ethan, and the other rebels. So much was at stake. His pulse was marching double-time. "Damn it."

Thomas struck again, the booming deep, mixed with a sharp snap of steel. First one free. He beat against the next girder, harder. Groaning followed but the second support held. Was that enough? A new quiet pulled him from his task and he paused. The rifle fire had stopped. He turned back to the hills, unable to make out anything with certainty.

A loud click came from above.

"I think I'd like it if you stopped that now." Prince Julian leant over the edge of the bridge, revolver trained on Thomas.

Chapter 23

On solid footing now, Thomas faced Julian across the centre of the bridge, his own weapon drawn as he circled away from the prince, now free of the rope. Julian shouted orders for his men not to fire. Thomas pulling his own gun had caught them off-guard but it was still a stalemate.

And Mia was right.

While a fair share of Williams' soldiers lay stricken around the vehicles, Thomas feared it was Ethan's men who faced the heavier losses. A second force of the king's troops had been hidden somewhere nearby, and they'd almost wiped out the rebels if the small group of prisoners huddled against the rock wall was any indication.

Had Silas betrayed everyone?

Or had Julian and his father simply been cautious, prepared after the mine attack?

Thomas had no answer, and truly the question didn't seem very important. Rifles were trained on Thomas but it was Ethan that kept him compliant – the prince held the barrel of a snub-nosed revolver to the rebel leader's temple.

Fury had drained Ethan's face of all colour but he did not struggle, though his eyes roved to his men often.

"Let him go and I will return to the city with you," Thomas said. *And lead you away from Mia.*

Julian raised an eyebrow. A fading bruise covered his throat. "Bargaining? My, my. How utterly ridiculous."

Thomas frowned. "Then I shoot you now and none of your men will retaliate – you can't afford to lose your pilot."

"I don't believe you will; even now my men are closing in on your sister's hiding place. And while they have orders not to kill her, those instructions certainly do not extend to refraining from hurting her," the prince said. He reached into an inner pocket of his jacket and withdrew a pocket watch. *Of course.* Julian flicked the lid open with his thumb. "And I'm giving you one minute exactly, to throw down your weapon."

Thomas lowered the barrel but did not drop his gun. Julian was bluffing. He had no idea where Mia was. If he had; he would have swept in before the failed raid. *But can I be sure?* "Don't try your serpent's tongue on me, your highness."

Julian only shrugged, eyes on his watch. "Forty seconds."

The watch had to be the key – but how? Did it bear a likeness of the moon? Thomas couldn't very well ask. And he was running out of time. Steel creaked but still the bridge held. But for how long? It was dangerously close to collapse – he could feel the strain, the weight, the desperation for steel to hold together – it pulsed up through his feet. *As if I'm connected to the bridge somehow.* All that weight, the copper, the steam car crunched into the rails behind Julian.

The bodies, the men and their rifles. So many gathered

on one side of the bridge.

"Twenty seconds – you need to decide, Thomas. Don't let another woman you love suffer at my hands."

Leah.

Mia.

Thomas ground his teeth. *Focus! You have to turn the tables here.*

Maybe if he simply shifted his weight, would it be enough?

Thomas raised his hands slowly, keeping the gun high, nose pointed toward the sky, finger off the trigger. He took a single step forward. The soldiers around him tensed. How exposed his chest and back felt now – just a single anxious squeeze of the trigger and a dozen rifle rounds could tear into him.

But Julian only smiled. "A wise decision."

Thomas took another step, lifted his foot for a third – and a screech sliced through the air. It was too much. The remaining girders finally cracked.

Saint's Bridge tilted sharply.

Men lost their footing, plunging over the rail with cries of shock. Steam-cars followed, crashing against the rail before splashing into the river below. The prince was suddenly scrambling for purchase beside Ethan; gun and watch forgotten – glittering as they plunged into the water.

Thomas was already leaping after Ethan.

He hit the water, cold enveloping him. A storm of bubbles obscured his vision as steel continued to plunge into the water around him. The mess of bubbles eased enough for him to shove at a jagged piece of support beam, twisting around it before the thing impaled him. A deep, muffled boom crossed the river as something enormous settled.

He broke the surface; spinning. The bridge towered over him, even as the current drew him toward it. Two sides dipped down toward the river like twisted prongs. A body hung from the wreckage of the railing.

Faint cries for help reached him – shapes bobbed in the water ahead. Was that a glimpse of blue from Ethan? And Julian, had the prince survived? Thomas swam for the blue but the current pulled it under and out of sight. "Ethan!"

Thomas splashed forward, only to thump into something hard. Winded, he scrambled for purchase on the submerged stone. Ahead, there was no trace of blue clothing anymore. Thomas caught his breath, hesitating. If he let the current take him, who knew where he'd end up? And Mia needed him; if Ethan had survived, he was alone now. "I'm sorry," Thomas said.

He swam back toward the bridge, fighting the current until he caught a piece of the wreckage. He started to climb, only to slip and crash back beneath the surface. Something bright glittered beneath him. The pocket watch? Thomas twisted, kicking hard. His lungs were already beginning to tighten, but he kicked a little deeper and there it was – resting atop a sealed crate.

Thomas' hand clamped around the watch before he twisted to thrust himself up, using the crate as a platform.

The surface quickly resolved, growing brighter as he clawed his way back.

Breaking free, Thomas sucked in great lungfuls of welcome air, treading water and blinking his vision clear. The wreckage was still close enough to reach. He angled toward the nearest point where the bridge hit the water and with his free hand he caught one of the rails. His legs were pulled toward the first bend, but he took a moment to check the watch face – a moon! Without examining it further, he slipped the watch into his pocket and started to haul himself up the ruined bridge.

This time he took more care, letting the warmth build in his body. His hands should have slipped more often, but he found the grip easy enough – almost as if his fingers sunk into the steel, creating grooves – and when he was finally standing on the still-creaking end of the bridge, he was surprised to find his balance had improved enough that he could pause to scan the river. *Another facet to Silas' gift?*

Still no sign of Ethan or Julian. Bodies floated downstream, bumping into one another, occasionally getting caught on some manner of underwater snag but none waved for help. Across the remains of the bridge Williams' men had lined the banks. Several were working with rope while others simply stared, rifles held only loosely.

Damn this – how do I deal with them? Thomas started toward the group. He held no weapon but did he have a bargaining chip after all? Could he convince them he was as important as Julian and Williams claimed? The only other option would be to return to the water and try his luck reaching a bank downstream, and the sides were steep for who knew how long? He could also try to swim to the other side of the collapsed structure, maybe circle around to Ethan's camp from the north.

But leaving the prisoners behind... could he really do it? Knowing that they'd be slaughtered – or possibly worse, enslaved.

Thomas continued forward.

The first soldier to notice him lifted his weapon, a willow rifle. "Stop."

Thomas kept walking, nodding to the captured rebels. "You're wasting time with us – think Williams will forgive the death of his son if you present him with me and a handful of rebels?"

The man said nothing, but a fellow with a sergeant's stripes joined the first. He held a twin-shot, the heavier gauge enough to blow Thomas' head clean from his shoulders at close range. Thomas fought the urge to swallow or take a breath.

"Surrender, Thomas," the sergeant said. "We hold the upper hand. You know that."

"You hold nothing if Julian has drowned. On the other hand, if he's washed up on the banks downstream, on the verge of death and you save him..."

"I already have two-score men searching." He spat. "You're out of options."

A shot rang out and the sergeant collapsed.

Thomas dropped into a crouch. The remaining soldiers swung their rifles toward the surrounding hills, some toward the road too, but a hail of bullets cut them down and suddenly there was silence, save for the twitching of one man, boot scraping on stone.

When the sound finally ceased, Thomas straightened to turn toward the direction of the gunfire. Above, near the path Thomas and Ethan had used, stood Genevieve – magnifier rifle in hand – and beside her was Mia, her blindfold bright beneath the sun.

Chapter 24

Fire burned low in Ethan's camp, doing little to hold the darkness at bay. Torches were lit and the sound of tents being broken down continued to wash over Thomas; hushed tones and careful stacking and arranging, gravel crunching and rifles being loaded, checked and re-checked. Even the usual simmer from the central cauldron was absent – he held cold meat and coarse bread where he sat with Mia and waited for Genevieve and the scouts to return.

He examined Julian's pocket watch once more while he did; the smooth edges of the circular piece worn with age. Older than Thomas had at first thought. The numbers on the face were written in a rigid script much simpler than the flowing, lavish script currently used. It may have predated the Williams' line and their usurpation of the nation.

Twice he'd described the face to Mia but it triggered no more certainty about the watch than she'd already been afforded by her gift. The moon was a textured surface beneath the glass lid, the slightly raised hands made from bone. He planned to unscrew the backing when given a chance, but hadn't the heart to search for the tools after the failed raid.

The back of the pocket watch did bear an inscription, but it was in no language he'd ever seen.

"I hear them," Mia said.

Thomas stood, rifle in hand – but Mia was right. Genevieve and her two scouts appeared in the light, faces weary. "Gather by the fire." Genevieve waved an arm.

The fifteen or so rebels who remained were made up of those who survived the disaster on the bridge and those who had stayed to protect the camp. Others from Ethan's force of one hundred were even now searching the river for Ethan, risking capture from Williams' own search parties. Genevieve had told him to rest, that he'd done enough for now. One of the survivors must have told her about his attempt to find Ethan, though he couldn't shake the feeling that he could have done more.

But Mia had to come first.

"We found Benjamin, Carlo and the others," Genevieve said. "No sign of Ethan – but they found several sets of tracks to suggest a few people at least, climbed from the river. They're still looking – and they want to keep looking until they find him."

"Can't stay out there forever," a stout man said. He tossed a thin branch into the fire. "Williams' will catch them; we should bring Ben and Carlo back." Murmurs of assent followed and Thomas found himself agreeing though he did not feel it was his place to speak.

"I tried; neither will listen," Genevieve said. "And you all know what Ethan expects us to do: the second location. Right?"

Nods around the fire.

"What's that?" Thomas asked.

"Ethan had a secondary plan for everything. There's another hidden camp to the south. We'll take you there if you want to continue on your search," Genevieve said. Her voice revealed no sense of what she desired.

"Thank you. I think we'll decide once we're a little further from Williams' reach," Mia said.

"Of course." Genevieve looked to each face. "Whether Ethan is able to return to us or not, we struck a serious blow today. He'd be proud of us, all of us, even Thomas and Mia, who took the same risks we did."

Again, the group murmured its assent, one man reaching out to clap Thomas' shoulder. Someone thanked Mia for the warning that convinced Genevieve an all-out attack was needed, allowing them to save at least those who'd been taken prisoner.

"I know we need to do more," Genevieve said. "And we mourn much, but don't forget we've set back Julian's war-machine by weeks, giving us valuable time to plan our next strike. And more, we may have killed Julian himself, something which would cripple the King's plans."

"I won't believe it until I spit on his corpse," one of the rebels said.

Genevieve nodded. "I know. We can't assume he's dead, but we can hope. All right, let's finish up and get moving."

Once the camp was packed and snake-lanterns lit, the vastly smaller force – heavily burdened – started through the hills. Thomas guided Mia as best he could, but after a while it was clear they wouldn't be able to keep up so he lifted her into his arms. "I don't want to be a burden," she said.

"And I don't want to leave you behind."

The path eventually grew more even and the moon appeared – a huge white eye watching over them. The trail Genevieve used mostly ran parallel with the King's road, only it was at the mercy of the landscape – thickets of trees and rivulets or streams, undulating ground, but all were traversed with little grumbling.

Being tired and alive is always better than being dead.

They took several breaks and only once came close to discovery; a hissed whisper flitting down their line to reach Thomas. He came to a halt, setting Mia down. While she was by no means heavy, it was still a long trek and his arms were weary. A slight fog had been building as he'd marched but it disappeared the moment lamplight flared close by.

Voices shouted to one another, a co-ordinated search.

"We've already been over here," one man said.

"I mean a proper search, Anderson. Did you even leave the damn road?"

The first man snapped back. "Don't be a bastard. Yes, we did. Hours ago – there ain't nothing out there."

"Fine, come in then. We'll head back toward the river."

The voices faded, along with their argument. A good omen. Thomas started along the trail with renewed energy. *Still, I hope we're nearly at the second camp.* By his estimation they had slipped Williams' net. Search parties in the south were pushing in toward the city, assuming that the ground they'd already covered would be empty.

It didn't bode well for Benjamin and Carlo's men or Ethan if he'd survived.

Before dawn they came upon an underground cavern,

its opening concealed within a grove of trees whose roots appeared as nothing more than pale, clogged hair. Yet they were thick and plentiful, helping make a good hiding place, save for the stagnant scent of the nearby marshlands. Of course, the southern marsh wasn't all bad – he'd seen beautiful flowers and gentle creatures in the past. As a young man he'd been forced to help the nobles hunt the very same creatures on the edges of the marsh.

Further in, it grew dangerous with deep pools and poisonous things, but the old Southern Highway would eventually lead into Viterra's Wastelands and, hopefully, their best chance at freedom. Thomas frowned, even as he spread bedding in the cool underground. *Ethan and the others would say the best chance was something else entirely.*

Yet the rebellion wasn't the way for him and Mia.

It was too great of a risk; he knew that.

"Thomas?" Mia asked from where she lay beside him. A single lamp burned, its oil slightly sweet. The cavern was well-appointed, weapons and provisions appeared at the limit of the light – toward the back of the cave – where sleeping nooks had been dug out of the walls. Not quite enough for all of Ethan's men before the raid, but enough now.

"Are you cold?" he asked. "I don't know if there are any more blankets. They had to leave a lot behind."

"No." She lowered her voice. "I just wanted to thank you. For carrying me all that way."

"You don't have to thank me."

"Yes I do – it's important, Thomas. What kind of sister would I be if I didn't?"

He smiled into the dark. "I know you appreciate me."

"Good, because I do. And stop smiling, I'm being serious."

"I know. And I am too when I say that I know." He turned onto his side. "Now how about we get some sleep? Tomorrow's likely to be another long day."

"Do you remember much about the marsh?"

"Enough to avoid the worst of it, I think – just let me know if you sense something and that should cover the rest."

"I will."

Chapter 25

Genevieve saw them off late the next afternoon with new provisions and weapons, along with some of the supplies Ethan had obviously specifically gathered for the possibility of fleeing into the marsh – including insect nets, a kind of thin tent designed to protect travellers from all manner of fevers and bites, which was something Thomas was most grateful for. Aside from the poisonous bites, there was a particularly annoying gnat with sticky feet that caused no shortage of irritation.

"We hope you find him," Thomas said to Genevieve. "I wish I'd been able to."

She nodded. "And luck to you in your quest, the both of you."

They started deeper into the mangroves, following an old road, falling sun casting long, twisted shadows. The scent of stagnant water and damp earth was strong. Overhead, the occasional warbling squawk of dragon-birds filled the groves. Thomas spied one as it leapt from tree to tree, its over-sized claws gripping the branches and scraping away bark. The sharp talons were used to dig through the mud to find worms, grubs and other food, though he'd seen one attack a hunting party that neared its nest.

"What's that sound?" Mia asked. "It sounds like no bird I've heard before."

"It's a dragon-bird," Thomas said. A red feather drifted down to the murky water, vivid against the surface. A sickly rainbow ripple spread from the feather. Oil. Polluted by Birnhale somehow? It didn't seem to be the slow rot of the marshes itself. The bird ought to have been brighter still; there was no sheen to the wings. "He's a strong red and his claws are almost too big so he can't fly very far. They usually stay in the tree tops when they're not eating."

"Truly? A bird that colour… I didn't think such birds existed anymore."

"When we were younger and the lords took me on the hunts, they'd trap the dragon-bird to use its feathers to ornament their hats."

"Typical," Mia said.

On they walked, following the faltering stonework of the sunken road. The pavers beneath Thomas' boots were cracked with age, stained or even missing altogether, but their path was even and straight enough. Where the road passed over spongy ground, or where the roots of the mangrove had crept across the path, they had been cut back in the past. Even the newer roots were not impassable. Had Genevieve been willing to part with the hidden steam-car, located a little further west of the second camp, it would have been a bumpy but hardly unpassable ride.

As it was, they were making good time. "There's an old hunting camp perhaps an hour away," he said. "We'll reach it before dark. It used to be an outpost so we'll have decent shelter."

"Can we risk a hot meal?" Mia asked.

"Probably," he said. "I don't think Williams' men will search here. They'll be too busy focusing on Julian or Genevieve to worry about us." He said it without allowing himself to acknowledge the twinge of guilt that followed.

She was silent a moment. "Do you think he survived the river?"

"The prince?"

"No. Ethan. Though I'd pray for Julian's death if I thought it'd make a difference."

Thomas sighed. "Maybe. A lot of people died on the bridge. I thought I saw Ethan but I can't be sure."

"Many deserved it."

"We may never find out about the prince. If we find the airship we'll be truly free for the first time in our lives, Mia. It won't matter then, at least."

"If the ship exists."

"It does – I've seen the photograph."

She touched his arm, stopping. "And if we cannot find it? If it's ruined? Broken?"

Thomas had no answer. He kept his voice even. "Then we deal with that problem when we face it."

"All right. Let's get to the outpost first."

It didn't take long to reach the winding path that led to the ruin and as Thomas had estimated, they beat the sunset. There had once been a proper side road but it had long since slid into the marsh, edges of stone peeking up from one of the larger pools. Tiny orange flowers grew by the water in berry-like shapes.

The abandoned outpost was but four walls of stone and a makeshift roof of roots and dried mud where more tiny orange flowers sprouted amid tangled green shoots. Thomas pushed the door open, silt sliding as he did. Inside, an opposite window let light within – set high where the stairs once climbed. But now, the stairway ended before the roof, its crumbled remains shoved beneath it.

Elsewhere, hints of order. A mostly clear space for bedrolls and a stone fire-pit with a cold grill. Dried logs, largely irregular branches from the mangroves, were stacked beside a row of boat hooks, their steel dull in the dim interior. His last memory of seeing them in action was of Julian dragging a large, floating clump of weeds and mud closer, so that the pale blue eggs of the heron could be collected.

Once they'd arranged bedding, started a fire and set water to boil, Thomas sat before the flames, Mia close by, and removed the pocket watch, taking his meagre tool set from the pack.

"Let's see." He flipped it over and set the thin screwdriver to the screws and twisted. Nothing. He tried harder, pushing down firmly, but it would not move. Try as he might, the casing remained closed. "Looks like we won't find any clues inside, since I can't open it," he said. "Unless you want me to break it?"

"No. Can I try?"

"Absolutely." He handed it around the flames but paused. "Wait." There was movement on the face, had the bone hands just shifted too quickly?

"Thomas?"

"The hands are..." he trailed off. When he drew the watch closer, the hour hand flickered, almost like a compass needle.

When he stretched his arm back toward Mia, the hour hand moved again before settling into stillness. Even the minute hand had twitched. "When I move the watch to the south, the hands move like a compass. But elsewhere, they act normally."

"We're meant to follow it," Mia said, conviction clear in her tone.

"Well, we're already heading south. That's got to be a good sign, doesn't it?"

"I think so."

The pot began to hiss. Thomas took it off the fire and poured the hot water into the cups Mia had arranged, the bitter scent of tea leaves rising. He let it cool while he toyed with the watch. *How did a fool like Julian end up with you? And why didn't he notice the hands?*

Maybe they didn't move for the prince.

Thomas took a sip and exhaled; the warmth spread through his stomach in a welcome bloom despite the mild evening. Sometime tomorrow he'd pass a point further than he'd travelled with the hunting parties and had to wonder just how reliable the road would be the deeper they went.

He knew the regular dangers of the marsh but there were also rumours of a hidden people here, people who did not care for outsiders. Folk who drowned strangers and hanged their bodies from the trees as a warning. Was it just an old tale? Or had such a people been responsible for the nobles' reluctance to travel too far?

Typical that he'd think of the stories now, as darkness pressed in around the outpost and tiny, unfamiliar sounds grew loud in the hush. The thin plink of insects dropping into water, the wind through the big leaves. So unlike the desert or the city.

Best not to put too much stock in rumours – after all, the ghost people of Marwin had not been real. Instead, they were an isolated group of runaway slaves and free-born. Thomas put his cup down. Had Elisabeth broken through to further terrorise Henry and his people? Probably not – Aiden was going to take them as slaves, they were probably on his ship or working the mine, miserable.

"I'm going to get some rest," Mia said, slipping between the insect net arranged over her bedding.

He nodded. "I'll watch first. Sleep well."

Chapter 26

Water lapped at the edges of the road where it cut through a lake.

On the far side, an enormous mangrove island stretched tall and wide, many of the canopies so large that they could have rivalled the finer, multi-storey inns in Birnhale. It stood dark, impenetrable – like a green city. It seemed to bear watching eyes of its own, though Thomas saw nothing to suggest it. Late afternoon sun cast beams through slowly scattering clouds as a wind stirred the water, ripples following. Something large and dark slithered just below the surface, but turned away from the crumbling embankment that, in places, was so eroded that the very stones were teetering. But in the centre of the Southern Highway, footing was solid.

He'd already warned Mia about the edges of the path but still he didn't start forward. Instead, he unslung one of the willow-rifles they'd taken from Genevieve and checked the bolt.

"What are you doing with that?" Mia asked.

"There's something about the island. I just get a... feeling from it."

"You're on your own this time," she said. "I feel nothing but weariness in the soles of my feet."

"We have to pass it anyway," he said. "I don't fancy a swim. Hold my belt; you should stay close."

He held the rifle ready as he walked, training it on the trees ahead but no figure emerged. At the mid-way point, the stones sunk a little beneath his feet and he hesitated, but the sponginess passed and he soon found himself standing before an arch of tangled roots, listening to the croaking of frogs. The arch led to a twisting trail, a diversion from the stones – the Southern Highway swallowed by mangrove.

"I might have to stoop," he said. "Watch your head." He took the first few steps. The green leaves and branches grew close, creating a tunnel of sorts, where only thin lances of light passed through. Yet the dragon-birds offered their odd call, and the sensation of being watched eased.

"I feel the shade," Mia said. "It's a tunnel."

"Let's see where it leads."

The path climbed and he had to help Mia traverse layers of mud and leaves and roots until the trail finally broke free into a small, light-filled clearing. An insistent squawking crossed the space from twin altars of steel – neither very tall – wedged in a pale, clay-like ground. Creeping vines grew nearer the edges of the clearing but they'd obviously been cleared around the altars. The squawk came from a dragon-bird, its feathered chest rising and falling slowly.

It had been tied down and it twitched at uneven intervals.

"Thomas." Mia's voice was full of concern. "Is there a dragon-bird here? Captured?"

"Yes," he said. "How did you know?"

"I hear her cries... I can almost understand."

He explained what lay before them, examining the trees as he did. There were at least half a dozen points where someone might pass through, not counting the trail opposite. But no sounds issued forth, no hint of shadowy movement. *I imagined the feeling of eyes upon us then.*

"I want to free her, Thomas," Mia said as she stepped forward.

Thomas caught her arm. "I don't know. It might be... I don't know, bait? Someone clearly tied it down."

"She's confused and scared." Her voice softened. "She's thinking of her eggs, left in a nest just east of here. I want to free the bird. We must. You should understand what it's like to be trapped."

Thomas muttered to himself, but said aloud. "I do."

"Good. Watch over me if you're worried."

He followed her across the clearing and to the altar, which her boot knocked before she came to a halt. Mia bent over the bird, her fingertips stroking its chest lightly. "It's all right, little one."

Twine held the dragon-bird in place, tied across the breast and at the ankles. The large claws were polished, sharp against the smooth altar surface, which was stained with old blood. Were birds the only things killed on the altar?

Mia took her belt knife and sliced the twine, one hand clamping the sharp talons down as she did. "Don't fret. You're free," she said, releasing the bird and stepping back. Wings fluttered and the talons scraped against stone as it sought its feet, movements unsteady. Its head snapped around, but did not find Mia – instead it faced the opposite trail.

A lean man stood within the tree line, an odd expression

on his face – something between a frown and a smile. His arms, face and torso were coated in white mud, leaving blue eyes bright against the paleness. He wore dark leathers also dusted white. From his belt hung a copper-blow dart and a spyglass. He gripped a heavy net in one hand and with the other, he pointed.

"You're not exactly what I hoped to catch, you know."

Thomas lifted his rifle, training it on the man. "Who are you?"

"A question I'd love for you to answer to be honest." The stranger did not seem perturbed by the rifle. "And I'm also curious as to how a dry-land woman can understand birds?"

"You trap the dragon-bird?" she said.

"Yes. Its cries often draw others near, making a harvest more plentiful. We use the claws for tools and weapons." His voice was calm, no apology offered for what seemed to be a simple fact of life.

"I'm freeing this one," she said.

"Something I am happy for you to do, if you will grant me some compensation for my loss."

"Such as?" Thomas asked, Mia's own question almost buried beneath his voice. The stranger still hadn't made any threatening moves and Mia had not indicated any danger, perhaps her gift had offered her no cause for worry.

The man chuckled. "Easy, fellow. I have no designs upon your lady, fair though she is. I am a proud father and husband."

"Sister," Thomas said. He didn't lower the gun but something about the man set him at ease. And it helped that Mia hadn't shown any fear.

"I see. Well, let me take you both to the Drinking Village

as I believe others would like to meet you. It is on your way south," he added when Thomas hesitated.

"Where we would be guests?" Mia asked.

He nodded, then added the words. "Yes. I am Adam. Please – we do not live like those in the city, those I assume you have fled."

"Lead on," Thomas said after Mia gave a nod.

Adam took them along a twisting series of paths, some through shallow, clear pools where tadpoles scattered from their boots and other paths over heaps of gnarled, twisted roots navigable via planks tied to stakes, without which, he would have had to carry Mia again. The sun was still warm whenever they broke free of the canopy, which continued to tower above them, casting shining light across the pools. Some were too deep to cross by foot but Adam took them across such water on floating platforms. Each was motorised with propeller and engine; they chugged through the water at a steady clip. Dark shapes shied away from the platforms, something which Thomas was grateful for.

"It's not far now," Adam said when they landed upon the most solid landmass Thomas had seen since entering the huge island. Giant mangroves towered high enough to cast deep shade and litter the ground with leaves so thick that footing became deceptive, almost like walking across damp blankets. His clothing was soaked with sweat and he had more than enough bites to drive a monk to madness but another platform appeared ahead, promising firm footing and, hopefully, a little civilisation.

As he climbed the steps after Adam, turning back to help Mia, Thomas blinked when a blue-legged crab scrambled up a tangle of roots, chased by a large black lizard with snapping jaws. A crunch followed and the crab twitched, legs flailing as it died.

The lizard slunk into the shadows beneath the roots.

Through the dim light, the walkway took them over a hill of root systems, in which, if he fell, Thomas was sure he'd never be able to climb back out. The walkway then sloped down to a pair of mangroves so tall and broad that each had openings doubling as guard posts cut within.

Steel gate posts were crossed above, permitting entry to what had to be the Drinking Village – though it didn't seem to be named for a fondness for spirits, if the two men who met Adam were any indication. They were similarly dressed to Adam but wore leather vests. Their hair was longer than Thomas was accustomed to beyond the nobility, tied at the back of the neck with pieces of twine.

The lead man frowned at them all, lifting a rifle with a dragon-bird talon affixed to the barrel, like a makeshift bayonet, but only addressed Adam. "This is a bad omen, Adam."

"A fine welcome, Lester. I know I'm empty-handed, but I've had worse luck."

The man glared. "That's not what I meant and you know it. Outsiders are trouble, they always are. Remember the last time–"

"The last time was a full three years before you were born. I'm taking them to see Edwina."

The man set his weapon aside to fold his arms. "It's dangerous."

"She can understand birds," Adam snapped. "Now let us in."

Lester blinked and the other man gasped, but both

moved aside. Adam hurried into a clearing of dappled sunlight. Men and women, all dressed the same as the guards, moved from huts made of mud and giant leaves and stalks or sometimes cut into broad trunks. Chimneys smoked, and huge frog-like braziers glowed – adding to the warmth, though they provided a sharp if subtly sweet scent too. Something to ward off the gnats?

Children played, running across the broad opening, chasing one another with painted sticks, which seemed to have a complex set of rules as far as Thomas could see from the game he half-observed while following Adam deeper into the village. Some folk watched them pass, worry clear on their faces. Adam would say a few words about taking Thomas and Mia to see Edwina and most people seemed to relax.

"Is Edwina in charge here?" Mia asked. A child stumbled along beside her for a short time, staring up at her blindfold, before running off.

"No, she is an old guest. We have a council. It is nothing so organised as the political structures of old, but it's more fair than Williams and his ilk."

"And she'd like to meet me because I was able to understand the dragon-bird?"

"I've no doubt she's also rather hungry for news of the outside lands. As am I, I admit."

"We're happy to share what we can," Thomas said. "And when we do, and when Edwina has spoken to Mia, will someone guide us to the southern edge of the marsh?"

"Perhaps me. If not, someone will help."

They passed more similar structures, people continuing to stare. None challenged Adam as Lester had but Thomas noticed Mia turning her head, as if searching. "Something wrong?" Thomas asked.

"No, I just smell food. Crab meat."

Thomas soon caught the scent and his stomach grumbled. Ahead, a man was cooking crab on a spit, these having brilliant red and orange shells. His fire was fed by dried logs and what seemed to be dried reeds, drawn from a nearby supply. The fellow grinned as Thomas gazed upon the meat. While Genevieve had spared all she could, such travel-fare was simple at best.

Adam laughed. "Edwina will feed us if we ask, don't worry." He pointed to a home with a stone base, mud-brick built up and roof thick with roots and more mud. Smoke, almost lavender against the deep green and pale mud, slipped from a chimney. "Let's see how grumpy she's feeling today."

Chapter 27

Edwina was a middle-aged woman with piercing grey eyes, one arm in a sling and a tobacco pipe perpetually between her teeth. She only removed it to add more tobacco or to speak through a grimace, as if every word caused her pain.

And maybe it did – there were more than a few jugs of swamp-wine on her workbenches, by the fireplace, and even on the stove. A curtain closed off a second room, from which she'd staggered forth after shouting for Adam to go away.

Adam, of course, had opened the door and ushered Thomas and Mia within. "Edwina, believe me. You'll want to meet these two."

And now the woman was examining them as she fiddled with her pipe.

Finally she huffed, turning back to Adam. "A former Bruiser and a blind girl?"

Thomas resisted the urge to correct her. If all it took to pass through the village was some talk, even if it was about

Mia's gift, then he'd let the woman think whatever she liked. *So long as it's only talk.* Edwina had the look of a doctor or even an alchemist, with her rumpled coat and curiosity, and no-one was laying a hand on Mia.

"This is Mia and her brother Thomas. Mia can understand the dragon-birds," Adam said, speaking with some emphasis, as if the words were of importance.

Which apparently they were.

Edwina straightened. "You're sure?"

"Yes," Adam said. "She knew what the bird was feeling and even where its nest lay, all without seeing it."

"That true, girl?"

"You can call me, Mia," she said. "And yes. I don't know how."

Edwina reached for a pair of spectacles where they rested on a bench. "Very well. Then let me show you something, Mia." She rummaged around on a shelf, before drawing forth a tin box. She waved everyone to a nearby table and opened it. Within rested a small sheaf of papers, which she proceeded to read. "Listen to this. It's a history of the marsh that dates back to before the Coal War by forty or fifty years. It says 'I observed the men, women and children listening to the various creatures of the marsh, from the dog-sized lizards right down to the insects. One man even claimed to be able to understand the very mangrove trees, though I doubt this is true. Yet I did not doubt the people's ability to communicate with the animals. There was too much harmony in their interactions.' He goes on to detail other parts of his time here but what I found quite sad was the fact that Adam's ancestors could understand far more animals than he."

Thomas glanced at Adam. "You can understand the animals here?"

"Mostly the manticore lizards and similar creatures," Adam said. "Many of us can."

"Yet the ability is fading." Edwina replaced the papers, withdrawing another. "The hereditary gift fades with each generation. I've been researching evidence of older, primal abilities for twenty years now and you are the first outside this community that I have come across who can display similar aptitude. I must ask; was your mother or father born near here perhaps?"

"We cannot say," Mia said, her voice flat, but she leant forward a little, her interest piqued and Thomas knew he'd done the same thing almost without realising. "Our parents are dead; we never knew them."

"Oh," Edwina said, her tone more of disappointment than sympathy. "Unfortunate. Well, you must be curious – this place may hold some answers, and while I have hardly travelled the whole nation, this may be one of the only places that have preserved the primal ways."

"One of?" Thomas asked.

"There have always been rumours about the mountain region in what's now the Inland Federation but I was not able to locate those who supposedly dwell there."

Mia turned away, as if expecting Thomas' eyes upon her and offering a pre-emptive refusal to answer. She had long ago closed the topic of their parents, always seeming disappointed in Thomas when he continued to hope that information might still be won, that a piece of their past was possible to reclaim. *"David is the only thing that comes close to a parent, Thomas,"* she'd always say. *"Don't waste your time on them."*

But how do we know they abandoned us? Thomas almost said it aloud; he'd tried that before too and it made no difference. Still, lately, she'd seemed more open to finding answers again.

And now a slim clue, after so many years?

Edwina had lifted the second piece of writing. "This one speaks of another traveller who visited the marsh. They witnessed the communication in action, where a man saved a clutch of eggs from a lightning strike after being warned by his dog. The marsh-lander, when asked about it, supposedly claimed knowledge of over fifty languages and the ability to speak to many creatures. Sadly, nothing else was recorded about him, not even a name. Still, I'm closer than ever to understanding the gift."

"Why?" Mia asked. "It seems a strange pursuit for a noblewoman."

"Thank you for the compliment," she said. "And you are correct, I have little in common with the fools back in the city – in any city, for that matter. I must find a way to preserve such skill and knowledge before the machinery of the new world wipes it – and us – out once more."

"Once more? That doesn't make sense."

She waved a hand. "Very nearly, then. I'm exaggerating for effect. Some histories speak of a time where machines were vastly more sophisticated, of other forces – forces beyond gunpowder and steam. Oral histories claim even more, that the entire world has known more than one rise and collapse. Certain religions further suppose that it is humanity's punishment, to repeat the same errors time and—"

Adam cleared his throat. "Edwina, I believe Mia and Thomas wish to continue travelling south. Sometime this week."

The woman frowned at Adam. "Very well, let them go." She turned to Mia. "On your journey back, I'd like to talk again. I'm curious to see if you can develop your skills here."

"On our way back?" Thomas asked.

"That's right. Adam says you're heading south – there's nothing there but a wasteland, bitter and dying. When you've had enough of that, you'll be back."

"We don't intend to come back."

Mia nodded. "Despite my curiosity, Williams and his son are chasing us; they might find our trail eventually. We can't risk it."

Edwina sniffed as she refilled her pipe. "Don't worry about those fools, they won't come here. No reason – nothing for them to steal."

"Williams won't give up," Thomas said. "They want us."

"They can't come within fifty miles without us knowing about it," Adam assured them. "Now, how about I get you some food while you both rest? I recommend you stay the night and we set off early tomorrow. The marsh is no place for newcomers to attempt in darkness." Edwina was seemingly lost in another piece of writing so Adam took them outside and along the path to a quiet dwelling, a wooden door built into the body of a trunk.

"We have no place for travellers, since there are so few," he said. "The family who lived here left for the city some years past, so you will find all you need within. I'll return with food."

"Any chance some of that food might include crab meat?"

Thomas asked.

Adam winked as he opened the door. "I'll do my best."

A single room awaited, space for stove and table with chairs beneath a window and three cots alongside the opposite wall. "There's hooks on the wall and roof, as if they had a curtain once," Thomas finished his quick description for Mia. The wood grain gave the interior a warm feel, much cleaner than the stone, steel and grime of Birnhale.

Thomas set his pack and rifle down by the door then sat at the table. Mia was placing her own gear nearby. He stood, chair scraping, to guide her to the table but she stopped him.

"I'm fine, Thomas." Her tone hinted at frustration.

He sighed. "Don't snap at me because I still want answers about them."

She moved slowly to the nearest cot and lay down. "I'm sorry but it's hard."

He sat again. "Because we never talk about them?"

"No." She was quiet a moment. "Because every time I think I've squashed down the hope, *your* hope re-awakens mine. And I know that's a mistake; it always is. It just leads to more pain."

"You don't know that for sure."

"It has in the past, Thomas. That's enough to know what's due us tomorrow."

He didn't push. The same discussion had played out many times over the years. *Edwina's story is a thin rumour at best anyway.* "I'm not saying I want to turn around and head for the Federation, just that I'm curious about what it might mean. Why can you understand birds? And the Bird of Light, where does it all come from – don't you feel the same?"

"I assume Mother taught me the lullaby," Mia said. "You know that."

"Yes. But who taught her?"

She rolled onto her side, turning away from him. "I'm not curious today. And David would have told us if he knew but he didn't and he's gone now so we have to focus on escaping Williams, not the past."

"We do," Thomas said and left it at that.

Chapter 28

The edge of the marsh gave way to a barren plain of dust and grey stone. A thin line of trees on a distant ridge stood stark black against the slow-rising sun. The hiss of the platform engine filled the morning hush, the only other sounds that of Thomas' boots squelching in the soft earth at the water's edge.

Adam tossed Mia's pack. Thomas caught it and set it aside before reaching for Mia's hand, helping her down. As he turned back to the platform, ready to give Adam a push into open water, he froze. A dark shape was growing bigger beneath the water, hard, dark green ridges breaking the surface. Yellow eyes blinked open, regarding him with seeming placidness. Sharp teeth were visible when the creature's long mouth opened; yet it did not attack, merely slipping beneath the water again.

"What was that?" Thomas asked.

Adam chuckled. "I should have warned you. She'd been following us most of the trip, just keeping an eye on things, I suspect."

"She told you that?" Thomas asked.

"Not in so many words, but yes. She's a crocodile, a little like a big water lizard – and one of the reasons you don't want to try and travel the waterways alone."

"No argument from me," Thomas said. He gave the raft a push, and Adam used the rudder to turn the platform. He glanced back, raising his voice over the engine. "Remember what I said about the wasteland – watch out for the craters; don't travel at night. And don't lose my spyglass, I want it back whenever you return."

"We won't," Thomas called.

Adam waved and then began to recede.

Thomas shouldered his pack and rifle before guiding Mia onto firmer ground, circling back toward the remnants of the Southern Highway. Here it was still paved but dust and dirt covered most of the stonework. Hints of green clung to the earth but the longer they walked the more infrequent they became.

When they stopped for water at the ridge, the tree line thin and twisted, Thomas checked on Mia. They'd spoken little since last evening but she seemed well enough. She drank and replaced her flask, adjusted her blindfold, the fine yellow material still doing its job for the most part, it seemed. She hadn't complained about her eyes – nor had she ever in the past for that matter.

He opened his mouth to speak but took another drink instead. *Maybe I'm no better than Mia when it comes to dealing with hope.* His was almost gone now; her vision was not improving and nor would it. The gift from the Bird of Light was not so much a gift as a... token or a glimpse of a miracle.

"Say it, Thomas," Mia said from where she leant against

her willow rifle.

He had to smile. "So you can hear my thoughts too, I see."

"No, but I know you," she said, fondness in her voice. "Come on, out with it. What's on your mind now?"

"I think I understand what you mean about hope because I've been clinging to it ever since the *Esmeralda*. I thought your sight would be restored by now and I'm afraid to ask again."

She crossed the space between them, a hand outstretched to find his cheek. "That's because you know the answer. I would have told you if anything had changed. I don't think I've been given anything more than just enough to make some things easier and some things worse."

"Like?"

"Seeing outlines and shadows makes it easier to move about sometimes. And I just might turn out to be a better shot in the right circumstances, but I get headaches now." She shrugged. "What's worse is the way it almost makes me remember what I'm missing, like I'm *this close* to glimpsing real detail again." She held up a thumb and forefinger, an inch apart. "It's confusing because I don't know whether what I'm seeing is a vague memory of what something *should* look like or true hints from whatever my eyes are actually seeing."

"We'll find something in Europa or the New States, Mia."

"Maybe."

Thomas put his flask away and hoisted his pack. "Let's keep moving. We need shelter before darkness. I don't want to fall into one of the holes Adam mentioned." He scanned the horizon, shading his eyes with one hand. Nothing but barren plains to the south but that was where the airship was said to have disappeared. He checked their back trail and swore.

The faint smudge of dust clung to the skyline, appearing beyond the western reaches of the marshes. *Julian.* Or his father. Either way, it meant trouble. The cloud was nothing like what the sand-hog created but it spoke of vehicles. There was no guarantee the prince would stumble upon their path but nor was that a reason *not* to be concerned.

"It's the prince, isn't it?" Mia said. "How close? And how did that slimy bastard find us?"

"I don't know how, but if they choose correctly, they could be upon us by nightfall. Do you get a feeling?"

Silence. Then, "It's him," Mia said. "Which way?"

He removed the compass and faced the old road – the hands snapped around the moon to point southward. "The watch still says south."

"South we go then."

***

As the sun set, it cast a pale orange fire across the plain, the boulders and strange depressions they'd been coming across all day. Each was filled with a variety of stone, old mud and rusted machinery, as if the wreckage of some past battle or city had been swept into the sloping depressions by some fastidious giant.

Some openings spanned what had to have been half a kilometre each, the bent, crushed and decaying contents bearing no glisten of polished steel, no hint of colour beyond the dark blood of rust.

At the current crater, which had to have been at least twice as wide as the others, Mia broke the hush. "Another one? What happened here?"

"I once heard an old story. Julian was speaking to Elisabeth while I waited on their table; he knew I could hear and he was trying to scare me," Thomas said as they walked. "He claimed a mad general once slaughtered a city, burying it all afterwards, people, the rubble of buildings, machines, everything – and that the ghosts of the dead still roamed the plains, spectres that dragged travellers into the craters and impaled them on the rusted remains of the war."

"That can't be the only reason no-one ever comes this way," Mia said. "If there really is an airship out here, Williams or his father or grandfather would have searched for it long before now."

"I know. It's the land, little grows here – neither Birnhale nor Viterra bother with this place."

"Right. But what of the airship?"

"Something is here. You said the watch was important, it's urging us south."

"And I still feel that but it was Julian's watch."

"Not at first."

Mia shook her head. "I mean that if it was his watch, and if it *does* lead to the airship, wouldn't he or someone in the royal family have followed it already?"

Thomas frowned. "The hands didn't move until we were pretty deep in the marsh… as if whatever it points toward was out of range before that point."

"You said nobles used to hunt the dragon-bird. Julian might have seen the hands move."

"All right. If that's true and he did go exploring *and* it led him to the airship, why doesn't Williams have it now?"

"There are only two reasons I can think of and neither

are good."

"It's a wreck. I remember. What else?"

"They don't know how to operate it."

Thomas gave a slow nod. "That makes sense. Well, we have to find out if we want a chance to finally escape for good."

"I know," she said, softly. "I just don't want you to get your hopes up. I still feel that we're on the right path but I don't know why. Or how things will work out."

"Until you tell me otherwise, I'm plan to believe we're going to find it."

"Then let's get moving," she said. "Julian won't have stopped long so neither should we."

Chapter 29

Thomas found a ring of boulders nestled within a veritable garden of them, the heavy shadows comforting in the dying light. Before visibility had fallen, he'd climbed atop one of the rock formations, making sure he wasn't outlined against the sky, and used Adam's spyglass to scour the plains. The horizon was clear. Julian had stopped – but how much closer was he?

He prepared a cold meal only and they spoke quietly as they ate, slowly working through the fresh fish and crab. After which, it was the rest of Genevieve's travel rations before they'd have to forage. But it was water that Thomas once more found himself concerned with; there wasn't an endless supply in their packs.

"Let me watch first," Mia said. "I'm not tired."

Thomas arranged his bedroll, laying the rifle beside it. "Wake me if you sense something. Or hear anything."

"I will."

Thomas stretched out and stared up at the pin-prick stars, weariness dragging his limbs down into the bedding. Not unpleasant, really. *Tomorrow we'll find something. I can feel it this time. And maybe it's just my hope. Or desperation.*

He closed his eyes.

When he opened them again, Mia was shaking his shoulder. "Your turn."

He groaned but rose to a sitting position. "Anything?"

"Nothing."

"Good." He shuffled to the edge of their tiny camp, breathing in the cool night air and stamping his feet before climbing another boulder, using the waning moon. Once atop it, he lifted the spyglass and swept the area he'd last seen Julian until he caught a flicker of orange. *Much closer than before.* The remains of a campfire or a trick of his tired eyes? At least there was no sound in the night, no sign that Julian was pressing on.

At dawn Thomas woke Mia, telling her how much ground Julian had gained. Her lips tightened but she pressed on, following the unwavering hands of the pocket watch deeper into the wasteland, rising sun banishing the lingering mildness of the night. It was good to move again despite the pressing danger – the sense that he was nearing their destination grew stronger.

It put a new firmness in his step.

But a rising cloud of dust and the flash of sun on metal put an end to the feeling too soon – he traced their movement with the spyglass, lowering it with a string of curses. "He'll cut us off if we keep heading south."

"Then he knows where we're going?"

"He must. We need to move faster – let me carry you for a time."

"And my pack and gun? It's a lot of weight, Thomas.

There's no point exhausting yourself."

"I don't want to dump any of it either." He clenched his teeth. She was right. And how much extra ground could he really cover, that way? "Hold my hand."

He set off at a jog. Whenever Mia stumbled he kept her upright. The rocky ground, now no more than a suggestion of the Southern Highway, flew by beneath them. They bypassed more craters and with each trip, the line of dust – Julian's steam-cars, drew closer. Engines grew audible. Hope slowly diminished.

"We're too slow," Thomas said. The lead car was visible now, dust spiralling out behind it. It would only be a matter of minutes before they'd be found and there was a chance the prince's convoy had already sighted them with their own spyglasses.

"What do we do?"

"Hide," he said as he skidded to a halt before one of the craters. Like all the others, it was filled with rusted machines. This one bore twisted steel beams and cladding, cracked cogs and wheels, the spouts of chimneys too and even a huge boiler, its door half-melted. *What fire can melt steel?*

The thought was fleeting; he had to find a way down – the edges weren't too steep, but once in the crater, they'd be trapped. It was a risk. Yet if Julian passed on...

"Thomas?"

"Into the crater. Let me go first," he said.

"We'll be trapped."

"Only if they find us. They might not even search every one – there are at least half a dozen nearby," he said, glancing around. And what other choice did they have? "It's this or we keep going until they run us down. Unless you want to try and call the Bird of Light?"

Mia ran a hand through her hair. "What if it doesn't appear, like in the *Albion*'s hold? I need the steam-cars close; we'd be sitting ducks. No. I don't want to risk it. I guess we really have no choice. I'm sorry, Thomas. If it weren't for me—"

"Don't say that," he said as he climbed over the edge. "It's not your fault. Now take my hand, we'll be fine."

Mia reached down and together they half-walked, half-slid to the bottom, each step stirring dust. Thomas did his best to cover their tracks with debris but it was hard to tell how effective his efforts would be. He led Mia between piles of rubble choked with splintered wooden beams and corroded pipes. He found a puddle between shattered fragments of roofing tiles, sick with insect larvae and the darkness of rust.

"Stay close," Thomas said. Various pieces of steel, much of it jagged, protruded from the mess. Footing was hardly secure and his boots crunched over gravel and decaying machinery alike. At one point, a spring-loaded arm from a factory machine, its girth easily the equal of his chest, lay in their path. He lifted it, urging Mia through as he strained – yet it wasn't as hard as he'd expected, even with the rust sapping some of the mass. *Gently now, no need to show them where we've been by throwing this thing aside.* He replaced the arm carefully and continued on, wiping his hands on his clothes. Flecks of orange, red and black fluttered to the crater floor.

"Where are we going?" Mia asked.

"There's a boiler a little way further," Thomas said. "It's large enough for six people to fit inside."

They climbed more uneven debris and when he and Mia stood before the boiler door, it was none too soon – the crunch of wheels over gravel seemed all too close.

Thomas gripped the door and took a breath – the now familiar tingling spread through his arms – and pulled. Steel screeched. He froze. But the cars above had not stopped; they weren't close enough to hear yet. He pulled again, muscles straining, and opened the door with a grunt.

The dirty scent of coal and rust assaulted him and Mia actually gagged. But thankfully, there was no pool of stagnant water to add to it – and once he crunched his way across the coal, he saw why. A large hole rested in the corner, allowing rainfall to slip away. Still, closing the door wasn't going to make things more pleasant.

He helped Mia inside and swung the door shut.

Darkness followed.

His eyes soon adjusted to the faint light that snuck in through what few holes time had managed to corrode. None were so large as to cause a problem, but they illuminated enough when added with what found a way around the edges of the door, to see Mia. She had slipped her blindfold over her nose and mouth.

"It's not that bad,"Thomas said – and immediately wished he hadn't opened his mouth. The *taste* of the rust coated his tongue.

"It's bad enough," she said.

The sound of wheels had come to a halt somewhere above and muffled shouts followed. One voice rose above the others.

"Spread out and find them. They're nearby so you've got no excuses. If you fail I'll have your wives and mothers for slaves, understood? Get going."

Prince Julian.

"That confirms it," Thomas whispered.

"Did you doubt me?"

"Not really."

Time passed slowly in the darkened boiler. The search seemed to centre on other craters, since the voices faded at first. When they drew near once more, over an hour later, Thomas had shifted positions many times. Now he sat on the coal, rifle trained on the door and waited. If Julian opened the door he'd shoot the man and surrender.

Anyone else and he wasn't sure.

Surrender was still probably the safest option for Mia.

One group of men coordinated a search in the next closest pit but the heavy tread of soldiers nearing quickly became dominant. Two voices competed with the crashing of debris being cast aside.

"This is ridiculous," one voice said. "No-one would hide in here."

"Why not?" another voice, this one tired – or bored – replied.

Another crash and thump. "Because it's a dead end, right? We're wasting our time for that royal prick. I could be back in the city taking a drink by now."

"He's not a prick," the second man replied. "When our slave ran away, he replaced her with one of his own stock."

"Well pardon me while I kneel down and kiss his royal toes. He ain't done nothing for me." The voices were closer now, cursing as they wrestled with something – the broken mechanical arm?

Thomas gripped his rifle. Their fortune had finally dried

up; fate had resumed its usual role of saboteur. *God damn it, but that's not true this time. I shouldn't have brought her here after all; we're trapped.*

Something clanged against the boiler. He flinched, biting the inside of his cheek. Blood started to ooze into his mouth but he did not spit. Mia hadn't flinched, but she rested a hand on his shoulder.

"What about that then?" the second man asked.

"Looks rusted shut to me."

"Maybe. I can't tell if it's been disturbed or not."

"We just threw a hunk of steel into it; I'd say it's been disturbed."

"You know what I mean."

"I do but I don't care, Arn. I'm heading back to tell the sergeant we couldn't find anything in our quarter. I've had enough of this place already."

Silence followed. Thomas held his breath. They were going to leave...

Arn finally snorted. "The prince will just make us search again; you're going to get me whipped *and* have my mother in the factories."

"Fine. We'll look inside and then we'll leave. Happy?"

"Not until we're home," Arn said as twin pairs of boots approached.

Thomas kept his finger over the trigger and Mia's grip tightened on his shoulder.

Chapter 30

Mia's lips brushed against his ear, her whisper hard to make out over the sound of scraping steel from beyond as the soldiers worked to remove the arm from where it obviously blocked the hatch.

"Steal their clothing."

He couldn't reply, since Arn and his reluctant partner were already wrenching at the door. If Mia's plan was to work, he couldn't risk a shot alerting everyone else. Thomas crept forward, changing his grip until the butt of the rifle was pointed at the opening.

Light poured in. He leapt into it, shouldering the hatch into one of the men.

He swung at the dark shape before him, ramming the rifle butt into someone, a choking sound his reward. Thomas' eyes had already adjusted when he spun to jab the second soldier in the gut, the man just reaching his feet, cutting off a cry of shock abruptly. The sound hadn't had the chance to echo. Thomas leapt atop the fellow, wrapping his arms around the man's neck and squeezing until the stunned soldier went limp.

Thomas let go and checked on the other – while the other man might wake, this fellow was already dead, windpipe crushed by Thomas' first blow.

And my luck comes at the cost of their lives.

"They knowingly worked for a tyrant, Thomas," Mia said after repeating his name several times. "Don't waste too much pity on them."

"I guess not." He got to work quickly, stripping them of their black flak jackets and weapons belts, carrying revolvers and a pouch of bullets. Their rifles were no-where to be seen but he found helmets and pairs of goggles for both him and Mia. She tucked her hair into the helm as he wiped his goggles clean of dust. Next Mia stuffed her blindfold into her shirt before working on her own goggles.

"Think this will work?" he asked as he gagged then hauled the nearest man into the boiler. Was it Arn or the other one? No matter, really.

"We have to try."

The body of the dead soldier was next and then he shut the door, leaning the heavy arm across it. If the survivor woke, he wouldn't be able to escape and alert the others. *Instead, he'll break his way out or die of thirst in the dark.*

Yet Mia's words helped push the thought away. Both soldiers had chosen to be a party to slavery. One even owned a slave.

"Where now?" Thomas asked as he led Mia back the way they'd come. "I'm guessing your plan was for us to simply walk out of here, right?"

"Pretty much."

"Not south then?"

"Maybe circle around, act like we're searching another hole."

"Good idea."

At the crater's edge Thomas climbed free then turned back to help Mia. Once she stood beside him, she busied herself with checking her rifle while he glanced around, as if waiting. Two craters over, half a dozen steam cars stood beneath the sun. Each towed carriages, which were doubtless filled with water barrels and would also have carried the men they transported. Several dozen soldiers were spread across the wastes, usually working in pairs.

The nearest depression bore no soldiers and Julian himself was nowhere to be seen.

"Well?" Mia asked. Her goggles did a fair job of concealing her identity, when combined with the high collar and snug helmet.

"Nothing. We're pretty much surrounded but no-one's giving us a second look. I can't see Julian either."

"Then off we go."

"Think you can fool them?" Thomas asked.

"If anyone asks, just tell them I'm clumsy," she said. "Maybe they buy it, maybe they don't."

"Any feelings about this?"

"None. It's just you and me."

"Well, I've had worse company."

Thankfully, the ground was relatively even and Mia used her rifle as subtly as she could, preventing her from stumbling as they circled away from the searchers. The closest soldier stood some distance away and as Thomas neared, the man raised an arm and called across the pale stone.

"Any luck?"

"None," Thomas called back, trying to approximate Arn's flat voice – a difficult feat while shouting. *And while tense.* "Orders to widen the search."

"Right." The man turned back to his crater. Thomas kept on, resisting the urge to glance over his shoulder, something no soldier at ease would do. Instead he kept pace with Mia, as if bored with the search – something Julian's men seemed quite inclined to do. At the next opening in the earth, he moved around the perimeter until he knelt beside the edge and looked back to the others.

Still no indication that they'd been discovered. Mia stood nearby, sipping from her flask.

"They're still hard at work," he said. "I'm going to slip into this one to make it look like we're trying, but you stay here, crouch as if you're watching for me. That way, if anyone signals, it wouldn't be unreasonable that you don't notice at first."

"Right."

Thomas stepped down, sliding a little, but did not explore. Instead, he waited to the count of one hundred. "That's enough. This isn't so large that it'd take me much longer."

At the next crater he pushed down a growing sense of relief – they were damn close to escaping. Again, he mimed a search and again, no-one gave chase, no-one challenged them. By the third pit Julian's men were growing small and at the fourth a mild breeze swept in to mask the black figures enough that Thomas stopped to slap his free hand against his thigh. "We've done it."

"Don't say that until we're in the sky, Thomas," Mia said, though she was smiling.

He removed the pocket watch and changed direction,

heading for the faint impression of a hillside to the south of the empty plain. The wind rose, whipping grey dust and sand to sting his hands, neck and cheeks. He joined Mia when she re-tied her scarf to protect her face, tearing at the lining of his stolen jacket.

"This is getting bad," Thomas shouted after a strong gust drove him back half a step.

"Is there any shelter?" Mia replied.

The hillside loomed ahead. "Maybe." He drove forward, letting Mia trail closely so the wind buffeted him instead. When the dark shape resolved into a heap of stone, dirt and steel tossed together like an accident, they circled swiftly. The hill soon bore the brunt of the dust storm, allowing him to pause long enough to examine the rubble.

"We can shelter here," he said.

"Where is here?" Mia asked. "The wind has changed – is it a ruin?"

"More like a jumble of what was in the craters, but with more dirt. I think we can ride out the storm here."

"If this is the only shelter for kilometres then it's the first place Julian will look."

"Did you want to risk pushing on and hoping for something else?" Thomas asked. "There might be another crater nearby, I don't know."

"No. That might be worse. At least the storm will pin him down too."

"True." Thomas stepped into the rubble where a natural opening lay, more of a chance settling of pieces, really. "Stand back a little; I'm going to move some things around."

Mia did so and he got to work expanding the shelter, hauling stones aside and sheets of steel, mostly rusted like the rest, arranging them into something of a lean-to. Now unsurprisingly, perhaps, he was finding the steel lighter and easier to manipulate, he curved a piece here and there without too much trouble. *Whenever I finally speak to Silas he's going to have a lot of questions to answer.*

Chapter 31

When the wind eased enough to set out again – some hours later – Thomas checked the hands of the watch for 'south', then led Mia back into the pale, dust-cloaked world. This time he'd tied them together via a short length of rope, just to be safe. The swirls remained strong enough to provide some cover but his vision wasn't so impaired that he'd send them tumbling into a crater either.

He did bypass several openings on their trek, mentioning each to Mia. They seemed to be growing smaller. Light faded as the afternoon wore on. They'd stopped to eat, huddled together so as not to swallow too much dust, and then it was back to their southward journey.

The setting sun put an end to the wind, as if the great ball of orange fire had burnt it clean away, and now Thomas could see far enough to make out more hills before them, only these proved to be natural. Their sides climbed high enough to smother the orange sky. Well-trodden paths wove between the boulders and pillars of uneven stone, edges softened by generations of wind.

"It's like a maze," he told Mia. "Some of the walls appear to have carvings but I can't tell if they're natural or of a pattern far beyond anything I know."

"What does the watch do?"

"It still points south and one of the paths leads that way – we're on the right track."

"What about a place to stop for the night?"

"That we can find too, I'm sure." Thomas rested a hand against one of the stone pillars where it reared up as part of a trio. Each stood crammed together before an opening in the hillside. They blocked access for all but those on foot – a good omen if Julian did catch up to them. Assuming he'd chosen correctly and that the dust storm hadn't turned him astray.

Of course, the bastard found us once before easily enough.

"The hands point to a path leading into the hill itself," he said. "We have to follow it. The airship has to be in here somewhere."

"Shelter first – I want a hot meal if we can."

"Let's see," he said, and started between the pillars and into the dim passage, where he soon stopped to light their lantern. It cast a warm glow across the rough walls and in time, revealed paved stone beneath his feet. *Another sign. We might just escape once and for all.*

The passage had no sharp turns, it only gently curved its way deeper into the hillside, always to the right and eventually sloping downward too.

"We're walking a spiral," Mia said after a time.

He nodded. "I think you're right. Maybe the airship was hidden underground."

"Then I hope it has a skylight."

They spiralled further down, the walls never changing, the lantern light constant, bringing about a sense of timelessness. Only the growing weariness in his calves spoke of the passage of time, and the vague emptiness in his stomach. Above, the sun would have set long ago and when the passage finally levelled out to even ground he estimated that they'd descended easily twenty storeys.

At the end of the passage was a heavy steel door both twice as tall as Thomas and twice as wide had he lay across the floor before it. When he raised the lantern he couldn't fight a grin.

Engraved across the doors were a pair of crossed wrists, hourglasses clear on each, and a keyhole prominent in the sand.

"Gatehouse," he said. "Their symbol marks the door."

"Maybe the rumour was true," Mia said, her voice touched with relief. She moved forward to run her hand across the symbol. "The airship might wait behind this door."

He set his pack and lantern down before joining her, leaning against the steel. His skin tingled. "It has to be, doesn't it? You said the watch was important and it led us here."

"It did. But it could have led us here for another reason."

Thomas tapped his fingers against the cold surface. "Then *something* important is behind this door at least. Let's eat now, while we have the chance. Who knows whether Julian has followed."

Thomas knelt to unpack water, salted beef, bread and the last of their cheese, arranging it between them where they both rested against the door. "No stove," he said between bites. "Sorry." The food was filling if unspectacular.

"It's not too bad," she said.

Once they'd finished Mia yawned. It might have been enough to bring his own tiredness to mind – but it wasn't. He should have been bone-weary after the long trek, the strain of hiding, the persistent hope, but his pulse thrummed through his veins. He didn't want to rush but the urge to pace was strong. Whatever lay beyond the door, it wouldn't do to rush in. If Mia needed rest – as she should have needed – he could stand watch for a few hours. Dawn probably wasn't so far off.

"I can do sentry duty," he said.

"Shouldn't we push on?" Mia asked around another yawn. "What if they're right behind us?"

"If I hear them I'll wake you. Go on, rest," Thomas said.

"Just for a few hours." She started to spread her bedding, arranging the pack as a pillow and within moments her chest rose and fell in the easy rhythm of sleep. He turned the lantern down low and started up the passage a little way.

No echo of voices or tread of boots, nothing.

The watch passed quickly yet all he did was stand, listen, pace softly and sometimes examine the door. By the time Mia woke, reaching for her water before sitting up, he'd come up with an idea.

"No sign of pursuit," he said when Mia asked. "But I think I can open the doors."

"I didn't feel a keyhole or a handle before."

"The keyhole is probably part of the Gatehouse design – I think it would accommodate one of the handles found in Marwin."

"Well there's one back in Birnhale with everything else Williams took from us."

"I think I can break through if I try. You know my strength when it comes to steel."

"Because of Silas."

"Exactly."

She paused. "You haven't really talked about it, you know. We spend all our time on my gift."

He shrugged. "It's weird. My skin tingles when I'm near any piece of steel now. I don't actually know how I feel about it all; I can't remember what he did so it's almost like it never happened. That probably sounds stupid."

"Not really."

"Well, we must have been young."

"Maybe we should have tried harder to find him. He and Williams, they must have known something about our parents too."

"Once we get the airship, sis."

"All right then, let's see what you can do with the door."

Thomas braced his legs and put both hands on the door then pushed. Nothing. He pushed harder and the door creaked but held fast, but that was just the first test. "Something strange, even for me, happened on the bridge you know. I gripped and I could have sworn my hand started to slip *into* the steel. I think it had to do with friction."

"And now?"

He started to rub his hands together. "I'm going to try get the same effect from rubbing my hands." The tingling increased – but oddly enough, heat did not. Instead, it seemed a new energy built within his hands. *Like two elements reacting to one another?* The longer he worked at it the stronger the sensation became, gradually becoming unpleasant, almost sharp. When the feeling was near-unbearable, he placed his hands back against the wall and pushed.

His fingers sunk into the door.

"It's working!"

He kept the pressure on until his whole hands entered the steel, where he gripped the edges of the holes he'd made. He tore them open further. The gate shuddered and screeched as he worked, grunting with the effort. Sweat gathered at his temples as he tore strips free, bending them back time and time again.

When the new energy faded he'd already made an opening several feet deep, passing the edges of a complex locking mechanism. He rested his hands against the surface and this time pushed. It buckled instantly. "We're nearly through," Thomas said, then swung his fist.

His arm burst through the steel – yet the jagged edge did not tear his skin – and light poured into the tunnel. Squinting against the brightness, he threw another punch and then kicked the scraps of metal free until there was an opening large enough to climb through.

"Ready to meet our fate?" he asked Mia.

"As long as it's with you, I am."

Chapter 32

Thomas let his eyes adjust to the burning white.

When they did, he found only a soft glow from an array of latticed skylights resting high above. Dawn fell through the glass and into a monstrous cavern where it shone over the most magnificent structure he'd ever seen.

The airship.

It near-to filled the entire underground; the balloon somehow still inflated above its support cables. The tan material bore the very same Gatehouse symbol but also names painted larger than life; Jean, Stella, Orville and half a dozen others. The slogan he'd half-seen in the photo album was simple defiance: *we will never be your property again.*

As in the old photograph, the body stood sleek but powerful, like a shark frozen in burnished armour. The portholes were all closed, their canons silent – so too the array of Gatling guns lining the rails, their sights catching no light.

From where he and Mia stood the engine room was clearly visible by the huge, jutting propellers – one giant blade still sharp, and other, secondary blades mounted slightly to the side. These were mirrored nearer the fore – for thrusting into a strafe? A long ladder hung from a lower platform, which was in turn connected to an arched walkway that extended out from a ten storey building, flat and featureless.

Freedom.

He could have sprinted across the stone; this was their hope. Found. Whole. Complete – ready to fly. Somewhere within either the building or the airship itself, would be controls to open the skylight. And once that happened, there was no way Julian, Williams or anyone could stop them.

Instead of running, he put an arm around Mia's shoulders and tried to describe the wonder he saw. "Whoever built it must have been a genius," he said. "I feel like it could lift off right now, at any moment."

Mia hugged him back. "You said the balloon is still inflated. How? Hasn't it been here for over a century?"

"I don't know. Maybe they had technology long-since lost."

"Let's find out." Mia urged him forward, smiling broadly.

He started across the stony floor, boots echoing. "Do you feel anything about this place? See anything about the ship?"

"So far nothing."

"Let's take that as a good sign then."

The ground floor of the unadorned building, which was itself built up against the wall of the cavern, bore no door but instead a tall arch that admitted them into a dusty-reception centre. A set of steel stairs waited off to one side, but more tempting to Thomas, was the steel cage opposite. Heavy chains were connected via what he hoped was a pulley system, high above, to a box and a lever located within the cage. *An elevator*. It was wide enough to fit half a dozen people or a large piece of equipment. It would be the quickest way up to the airship.

"This way, there's a lift," he told Mia.

"Is it safe?" she asked, once they stood within and he'd latched the gate closed.

He examined the chain and the cage itself, running a fingertip over the smooth surface. "Not even a hint of rust."

"All right."

Thomas pulled the lever. Chains rattled and the cage started up at a steady pace. He gripped the handle and Mia caught onto him. Somewhere out of sight, the counterweight was dropping, helping them on their way. When the cage neared the top he pulled the lever again and the lift slowed, coming to a stop level with the walkway. Before them was what appeared to be a sitting room, with leather seating scattered around, but he led Mia directly to the walkway and its ladder.

"Short climb ahead," he told Mia.

"Right."

Up he went, hand over hand, until he reached a hatch. He gripped the handle and turned – it opened with barely a squeak. Darkness above. He hauled himself up then helped Mia before re-starting the lantern. The glow revealed the bowels of the ship; little to see aside from giant rivets and shadows.

A second ladder led to a narrow passage, where he opened a porthole to look down upon the ground, far below. Light was spreading across the cavern floor; he could make out the entry point where he'd torn through the steel gate.

They passed closed doors now. He checked the first, and finding it empty, moved on to the next ladder. This one led up several floors and eventually to the decks where he passed the silent sentinels of gunposts, taking Mia directly to the ornate door on the bridge. "That's where we'll find the controls."

"For the roof or the ship?" she asked.

"I hope both, somehow."

He tried the door and found it unlocked. Little more than vague shapes lay within. He lifted the lantern, setting it on a hook in the ceiling. It swung a moment, casting shadows as he started to walk Mia through what he saw.

"There's seating toward the back and a console with stools and bench near the door. It's unbelievable..." he trailed off. "And I'm the greatest fool who ever lived."

"Why?"

He leant over the bench, one hand on the wall. There were so many dials, buttons, levers and gauges that he couldn't recognise even half of them. Some doubtless measured steam pressure but what purpose could the little keys hold? They were arranged not unlike a piano, their colours inverted. Other parts seemed to require interlocking wheels to be turned, possibly by two people, their handles cold to touch.

He was a fool because he had overlooked the single-most obvious issue of all.

He was no pilot.

Worse, there was probably no-one alive who could fly it; Jean and his crew were long dead. There were probably a hundred things that needed attending to before flight was even possible. *If* everything in the engine room alone was still in working order. "I am an utter fool."

"Thomas, what's wrong?"

"I was too excited," he said. "Too hopeful, too relieved to see the ship in one piece."

"You can't figure the controls," she said into the stretching silence left after his words.

He thumped the wall. "And no-one can either, no-one!"

Mia said nothing.

Thomas squeezed back tears. *Why did we have to come this close before failing?* He opened his eyes, jaw clenched. A square handle rested before him on the wall. He snapped it down. "Damn everything to hell."

Mia put a hesitant arm on his back. "Don't."

He hissed a sigh. The anger remained but he had to use it properly, had to focus it on escape. On a new plan, on finding a way to—

Something rattled.

He stepped back, as did Mia. Light sliced through the wall as heavy, armoured shutters rose, revealing glass windows. The control room appeared in true detail and the impossible nature of their task was driven home once more. The controls curved around the wall – it seemed at least three people were needed to pilot the airship. He moved to one of the consoles – something didn't match the smooth metalwork.

It was a corroded iron chain and lock, keeping a wide steering wheel frozen in place. Each link was the size of his forearm. The lock bore a red seal, he lifted it and swore. "We're truly cursed."

"Is something broken?"

"No. The steering shaft is chained up. I could break the

chains... but there'd still be no use without a pilot."

"There's something else, isn't there?"

"Yes," he said, voice heavy with defeat. "There's a royal seal on the lock. By the V next to the W, I'd say Williams' grandfather found this long ago."

"Oh." Mia stepped closer. "But they never figured out a way to use it, Thomas."

He nodded absently as he slumped in a pilot's chair. "And neither can we."

She moved to his side, feeling for the second chair. "Don't give up yet. We might find something – let's search a little longer. I can't believe that Jean and the rest of Gatehouse would go to all the trouble of hiding the airship and then not preparing for the future, in case something went wrong."

"Maybe."

"Come on." She stood, tugging on his arm. He followed her up, then tried the door in the rear of the room. Captain's quarters? A twin bed and an empty wardrobe and desk. Charts covered the desk, many showing much older configurations of the nation. The Inland Federation was simply the Western Grace back then.

"Thomas, can you help me?"

He joined Mia, who held forth a journal with a crumbling spine. He opened it gently, rotten glue fragments falling to the floor. Most of the pages had been torn out, but toward the end, a sturdy script remained. Some of the words were a little archaic but he managed. "It starts in the middle of a sentence. It says, 'and so I hath pulled the ruby-red heart from Her and bequeathed it unto Arthur, Vivian's eldest and sent the lad away with all my knowledge... such is my shock at her betrayal that this is all I can manage, now that they are coming. But let them try and fly her without it.' There's no signature."

"Read it for me again." He did so and Mia was quiet a moment.

"You think Jean wrote it."

"Don't you?"

"Yes. And it sounds like he was betrayed. One use of 'her' bore a capital letter. The other did not."

She stood. "It also tells us why Williams' grandfather could never use the airship. They needed the ruby-red heart, whatever that is. And someone took it, along with the captain's knowledge. Presumably they escaped."

"So we need to find Arthur's line?"

"If the knowledge to fly this still exists, who else?"

Thomas straightened. Hope had wormed its way back into his chest. He swept Mia up into a hug and spun her around. "There's still a chance!"

As he swung her, something slipped free from her shirt.

A red key on a silver chain.

Its shape was not too dissimilar to a heart. He set Mia down, holding his breath. Could it be? "The key."

She held it up, lifting her blindfolded face. "Aiden gave this to me. Do you think…"

"Try it."

In the control room, Mia found the lock and fitted the key, only to let it clank back down when it didn't fit. "I thought we were on to something."

"Wait," Thomas said. He rubbed his hands together until the sharp tingling began, faster and faster until it hurt, then swung his hand at the chain in a chopping motion.

Two halves clattered to the floor.

His hand had passed through like carving butter with a knife.

Thomas tore at the chain until the wheel was free, then clenched his fist in triumph. There, resting in the centre of the wheel waited a red, vaguely heart-shaped keyhole. "There's another lock," he said.

Mia knelt beside him, raising the key to the wheel. It slid in perfectly. A click followed when she turned it. Gears shifted within the console and needles on the nearest dials jumped.

But Mia flicked the key back, tore it out and stuffed it back within her shirt.

Thomas gaped.

"Thomas? Sweet Mia?" A sneering voice echoed from below. "I think it's time you surrendered yourself to me, don't you? For you are most certainly trapped like rats in a ship now."

Chapter 33

"How did Aiden get this key?" Mia asked.

Thomas looked across the decking. Somewhere Julian and his men were below; there wasn't time to figure it out. Yet the same question seared into his own mind. There was an obvious connection, but what? And why would Aiden give it to Mia? "We have to find a way to escape Julian first," Thomas said. "He can't have the key."

"I know. And we've brought him and it right to the airship. Do you have any ideas?"

"Nothing brilliant comes to mind." He paced the control room. There were probably dozens of places to hide on the airship but that was no solution. He gripped his rifle, knuckles white. "We'll be outgunned if we try to attack; I don't know how to get out of this."

"Is there another way from the cavern?"

"Wait – the skylight."

"We'd have to climb the balloon somehow. Can we reach it if we do?"

"If we're quick maybe. We'll make lovely targets if Julian's already surrounded the airship."

"If they're blind it won't matter," Mia said. "Come on." She pushed him into motion and he exited the control room, slowing as he neared the rail.

Far below, Julian stood speaking to a ring of men in black. He had perhaps half a dozen soldiers – whether he'd sent the others to search different parts of the waste mattered little. If the Bird of Light would not come, their six guns would doubtless defeat his and Mia's two – even if one of those guns happened to be a nearby Gatling, assuming the weapon still worked. Assuming it had ammunition. Assuming he could use it before being shot himself.

And I've no doubt Julian will shoot me just to subdue me long enough to get back to the city.

Even with the advantage of high ground it was a poor prospect.

"If I have to send men up to drag you down here, you will both regret that most keenly," Julian called once more.

Mia was already humming. The familiar melody did not tug at his memory as it might have, though perhaps their mother sang a different tune to him. Instead, he remembered Mia humming and singing it. To David while the man laboured for breath, to herself while they crossed the desert, while they waited for sleep those first few years fleeing the city or when she called the bird down on Elisabeth's men at the *Esmeralda*.

The tune grew in volume and urgency but no great creature of light appeared, swooping down upon Julian. Mia continued but nothing happened and she broke off with a curse. "I don't know why it won't come." Her voice was dark with guilt. "It should appear; things are just as dire as before."

"Don't blame yourself, we'll try climbing anyway."

Thomas tugged Mia into a crouching run, heading for the opposite side of the airship. He paused at the rigging. A steel-rope ladder led up to the balloon itself but there would surely be an uncomfortable stretch that left them exposed to fire from below. If he carried Mia, would he be able to move fast enough? *At least the bullets will be more likely to hit me instead of her.*

"Not another step."

One of Williams soldiers stood across the deck, rifle raised. It was a willow, not the more vicious two-shot but it would still tear through him or Mia. *Bastard probably started climbing before Julian called to us. That was just to flush us out.*

Thomas didn't move but he didn't lower his weapon either.

"Prince says you're coming back with us. You can either walk back or ride on a stretcher." The man grinned, revealing a missing tooth. "I gotta admit that I don't want to have to carry either of you all the way back to the autos but hell, I'll only have to split the shift if you make me shoot you now."

A second man appeared, climbing from the ladder with a grunt. The first soldier glanced back, keeping half his attention on Thomas. "Take the girl, right?" he ordered.

The new soldier nodded, crossing the decks quickly.

Thomas tensed. *God damn it.* Was surrender the best option? If nothing else, it'd get the key away from the airship. And maybe that was more important than his own freedom right now. They could plan another escape...

"Drop them guns now," the first said.

As the newcomer neared the soldier with the missing tooth, his hands flashed. A muffled shot followed. The man with the rifle slid to the deck, gun clattering. Blood pooled beneath the fellow, sightless eyes wide with shock.

"Thank me later," the second man said. He removed his helmet and goggles to reveal sandy blond hair and a grinning face.

"Ethan?" Thomas said. He rushed forward. "Ethan, how?"

"Don't be surprised to hear this but it's a long story. Come on, we have to work something out before too many more men come up here. Is there a way out of that building?" he asked.

"No. But if we climbed—"

"Signal them up," Mia said, her voice firm. She'd obviously recovered from her own surprise, since Thomas was sure she'd have mentioned any premonitions about their rescue. "If we don't stop Julian here he'll just continue to hound us."

Ethan fell silent. Thomas eventually gave a slow nod. He bent to lift the rifle from the dead man at their feet. "All or nothing then?"

"Fine with me," Ethan said. "I'll ask them to bring stretchers. We need to find a good vantage point. Open fire when they're cramped together in the cage maybe. And we can't forget whoever stays on the ground."

"Right."

Ethan replaced his helmet and strode to the rail where he waved an arm at those below. "Send up stretchers, will you?" His voice bore a remarkable likeness to that of the man he'd killed moments before.

"Are they alive?" The prince called up.

"If we're quick, sire."

Julian's orders rang out and Ethan watched for a little while before turning from the rail. "The prince is joining those with the makeshift stretchers. Where do we set up?"

Thomas pointed. "Focused on the ladder. We let them climb up and then all three of us take our shots. Mia and I will fire from behind the crates by the control room. Take the upper deck?"

"Will do. Good luck – and don't stop shooting until they're all down." He glanced at Mia before he moved away, a flicker of worry in his eyes. *Maybe Ethan and I aren't so different, despite all his bravado.*

Thomas turned to his sister. Her lips were pressed into a firm line. She had no doubts, and neither should he; it was the right thing to do. Julian would hunt them all across the lands. He was responsible for creating a machine fit only for death and destruction. The man was part of a corrupt, soulless dynasty of tyrants, he was an enslaver. Tormenter.

There's not a single reason to let him live.

"Point me in the right direction, Thomas," Mia said.

"Right." They moved to the crates. He shifted one slightly to allow for more room behind the barrier, then restacked them, concealing Mia for the most part. Next he set Mia and Ethan's revolver behind one, having her steady her elbows, snug in the narrow gap between the boxes. He leant over her shoulder and looked down the sight. The opening lay directly in her line of fire. "Hold true this way," he said, then crouched down, setting his back to another crate, his own rifle in hand but not raised. It would be some time yet before they took the lift and then climbed aboard the airship.

Ethan was already in position, hidden across from the ladder. His disguise might still be good for a few moments if he faced them, but the element of surprise was more important than further subterfuge. For now, he made no signal.

Thomas shifted. How long had it been? He tapped a finger on the gun and shifted his legs.

"Don't fidget so much," Mia said. "You'll tense up and ruin your aim."

"I know." He set the rifle aside and linked his hands behind his head with a sigh. "But this is different."

"It has to be. If it were a fair fight or if we were shooting in rage... I know that would feel different to what we're about to do but we don't have that luxury."

"You're handling it better than me."

"Maybe."

From below, the rumble and creak of the lift reached him. Not long now. Thomas slid the bolt back and checked the round. Then he removed the magazine. Only a few rounds left. If he didn't rush he could get off at least three shots, surely. Once it was spent, if he got the chance, he'd take the second rifle and empty that.

"Ready over there?" Ethan called softly.

"Close enough," Mia replied.

The lift was rattling closer. Muffled voices followed, along with the tread of boots on the steel walkway. Thomas lifted his gun, placing the butt against his shoulder. The weight of it brought him some measure of comfort, slowed his pulse a little. Everything would come down to whether or not they were noticed right away.

Now the sound of men inside the airship, clambering along.

Then voices drifting up through the hatch above the ladder.

He gripped the stock.

Most of the soldiers had to climb free before he fired. But he couldn't simply let them shoot first either, if even one man happened to notice them, half-concealed as they were.

"Be still," he said quietly. "Shoot when I say."

Mia nodded.

Thomas peered around, his unblinking gaze on the ladder. Two poles of steel appeared, clattering to the decks. A heap of jackets followed. *Come on.* He ducked away and looked to Ethan. The man, concealed from anyone using the ladder, had line of sight with Thomas. He shook his head. Not yet.

A grunt from the ladders. "Where's Leonard?"

"Just get up there and find him," Julian's voice snapped from below.

Ethan held up one finger. Then two. And in moments, three and then four. His hand hovered near his own rifle and then he leapt to his feet, weapon raised.

Gunfire echoed in the cavern.

"Now," Thomas cried but Mia was already firing booming shots as he twisted, jamming the butt deeper into his shoulder and squeezing the trigger almost before he saw the target. Yet a man with no flak jacket fell to the deck with a shout, another already down beside him.

The Prince was reaching for his own revolver, a snarl on his face when Thomas swung his barrel, working the bolt as he did, spent round clinking across the deck.

And then he fired.

Prince Julian flew from his feet.

Time slowed for just a moment before the man hit the decking with a thump.

He lay sprawled on his back, his black and crimson suit in disarray, whole body motionless. Thomas stood slowly, weapon still raised. "Wait here," he told Mia. "The prince is down." Had one of her bullets hit at the same time as Thomas' round? The last soldier was crumpling into a heap as Thomas approached, Ethan running across the boards.

"Careful, Thomas," Mia said. "There might be others."

Thomas reloaded as he walked, checking on the ladder, but no more soldiers waited below. Though doubtless whoever remained on the ground would soon be heading for the lift.

Next he moved to Julian.

The prince's eyes were closed, the usual sneer on his face missing. In the growing light from above, the man appeared paler than usual. Topaz glinted from the ring on his open hand. And now Thomas did reach for the thin scar beneath his eye – was this what revenge felt like? *Shouldn't I feel more than relief? It's anti-climactic.* And why didn't it burn away some of the shame he'd felt when they were younger, when Thomas had been driven to impotent rage time and time again.

Especially after what Julian did to Leah.

Or claimed to have done. Thomas had never been able to decide whether the man was lying in order to torment him, or telling the truth to torment him. Either way, not knowing had been all too effective.

And surely *that* was why the revenge felt so empty; Thomas would never know now.

Movement flashed and a shot cracked the air.

Searing pain tore into Thomas' chest. His rifle fell, hands suddenly too weak to grip, but the gun made no sound as it hit the deck. *Wait, shouldn't I have heard it?* The Prince was twisting around where he lay, lifting his revolver.

Another shot rang out – and that sound Thomas heard; it echoed endlessly around the cavern as darkness drew him down.

Chapter 34

Thomas opened his eyes to light.

Pain radiated from his torso. Someone was breathing hard – no, *he* was breathing hard. Each gasp seemed to tear a new hole in his chest. Tears slipped from his eyes. He raised a hand only for someone to take it.

"Rest, Thomas." *Mia.*

He squinted against the brilliance of the sun... but it was only normal daylight that passed through the windows of the control room. Within, it was actually quite dim. Mia sat beside him where he lay on the floor, something soft beneath his head.

"What happened?" he managed. "I thought he was dead."

"Julian shot you – he was wearing some sort of steel plating beneath his clothes. It protected him from the bullets."

Bastard. "Then, he got away?"

"No. Ethan killed him."

The second shot. *Good.* Thomas closed his eyes again, catching his breath as best he could before he answered. "If he shot me, how am I alive? I felt it right in my chest."

Mia stroked his forehead with her free hand. "You won't believe it, Thomas."

"Tell me."

"Ethan saw it. He said you were struck opposite your heart, that the bullet should have pierced your lung but it was like your body... rejected the bullet and that after you fell, the steel was just pushed back out of the wound somehow." She squeezed his hand. "I heard the gunfire and I didn't know. I thought..."

He tried to smile. It probably came out as a grimace. "Looks like it's not that easy to kill me."

"I don't think you're out of the woods yet, Thomas. You need proper bandages and medicine. Ethan is looking."

"Right." Thomas swallowed, sending more ripples of pain throughout his torso. Whatever Silas had done, the alchemist left out something important – Thomas still felt pain. Far too much. New sweat was joining the old at his temples. "Do we have water?"

"Here." Mia guided a flask to his lips and he drank, spilling some but swallowing enough to ease the dryness of his mouth and throat.

"So. What now?" Thomas asked between more water.

"Ethan tried to stop the man who'd stayed below but only wounded him. He got away; he'll be bringing reinforcements so we need to leave."

"Where?"

"Ethan knows a place we can hide and recover."

"I hope he has a steam-carriage."

"We'll get there, Thomas. I'll make sure of it," she said.

"I know you will, sis. You're even more stubborn than me," he said, this time managing a proper smile. "I don't know what our next step should be but I know what I want it to be."

"The alchemist."

"I *really* want to meet him now. I have to understand what he did."

Mia nodded. "He might know how to find Aiden too. It's a long shot but I can't think of any other way to find out where the *Albion* might dock next. That Bruiser *has* to know something about the key, about Arthur's line."

"Maybe back to Henry's jewel mine?"

"Not so soon, surely?"

"Or he might be in Europa. He could be anywhere."

"I know," Mia said. She sounded weary. "It's not as though going back to the city isn't already a big enough risk. We're mad if we try this, Thomas."

Thomas lifted the flask again, ignoring a fresh wave of pain. The room was growing unbearably warm as the day heated up. It had to be late morning already – either that or it was his body. *I guess it's working hard to deal with the wound.* "True. But Aiden owes us some answers too. He said we were the Alchemist's pets, he was surprised we didn't remember him – he knows far more than he's said."

"Then we're going to do this?"

"When I can walk again," he said. "And we won't be alone. I bet Ethan will help us; he's eager to strike back."

"True," she said, a hint of relief in her voice. "But what if Aiden doesn't know anything about the *Clara*?"

"*Clara*? Is that her name?"

"Ethan told me it's painted above the controls – I'm surprised you didn't see it."

"Well, I'm glad I know. And if Aiden doesn't know

anything about the ship, he'll lead us to someone who does."

"Are you sure of that?" Mia asked.

"What does your gift tell you?"

"Nothing – nothing about the airship or Silas or Aiden for that matter."

He replaced his flask with her hand. "Then it's back to hope."

A Note from Ashley

Hi! I hope you enjoyed *The Red Hourglass* and thanks for reading.

I'd like to ask if you could help me out by leaving an honest review of the book at your place of purchase? Long or short, bad or good, it all helps!

AND if you'd like to sign up to my newsletter [visit www. ashleycapes.com] you'll be the first to know when the next Slaves of the New World book is released. You'll also have first access to preview chapters and pre-release editions of the story, in addition to being automatically added into the draw for giveaways.

ACKNOWLEDGMENTS

Thanks again to everyone who helped me with this one – it makes the late nights worthwhile to have your support!

As ever, I'd like to thank my wife Brooke for her unwavering support but also my writing group, the Alchemists, along with my editor Amanda and also Nick Deligaris for the stunning cover image! Thanks also to Vivid for the superb typeset on the cover and to any one who took a chance on *The Red Hourglass*.

Ashley

ABOUT ASHLEY

Ashley Capes is an Australian novelist, poet and teacher. He teaches English, Media and Music Production, has played in a metal band, worked in an art gallery and slaved away at music retail. Aside from reading and writing, Ashley loves volleyball and Studio Ghibli – and *Magnum PI*, easily one of the greatest television shows ever made.

Visit his blogs at www.cityofmasks.com & www.ashleycapes.com or follow him on twitter @Ash_Capes.

Fiction

The Bone Mask Trilogy
1. *City of Masks*
2. *The Lost Mask*
3. *Greatmask*

Book of Never
1. *The Amber Isle*
2. *A Forest of Eyes*
3. *River God*
4. *The Peaks of Autumn*
5. *Imperial Towers*
0. *Never (Prequel to The Amber Isle)*